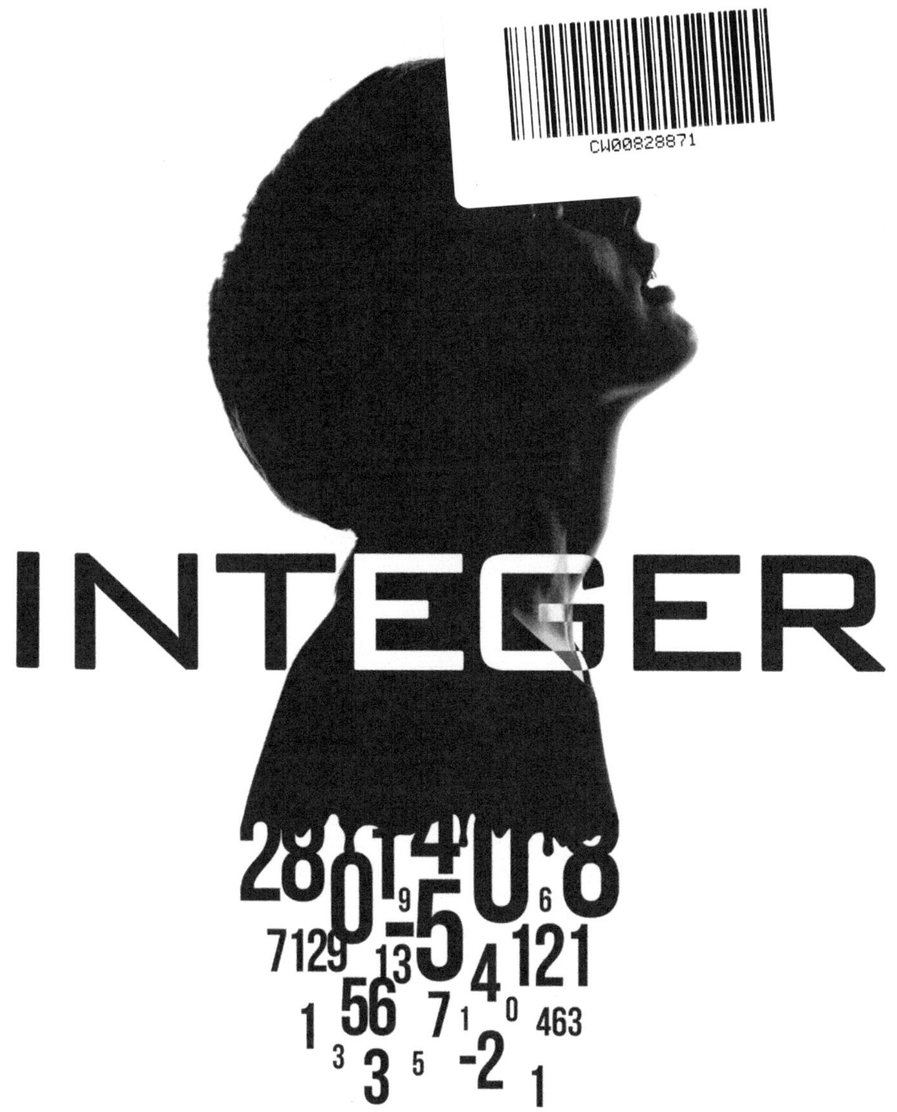

The Countdown Is On

Edited By Wendy Laws

First published in Great Britain in 2023 by:

Young Writers
Remus House
Coltsfoot Drive
Peterborough
PE2 9BF
Telephone: 01733 890066
Website: www.youngwriters.co.uk

Book Design by Ashley Janson

Softback ISBN 978-1-80459-401-8

Printed and bound in the UK by BookPrintingUK
Website: www.bookprintinguk.com
YB0536C

FOREWORD

For our latest competition, Integer, we asked secondary school students to take inspiration from numbers in the world around them and create a story. Whether it's racing against a deadline, cracking a mysterious code, or writing about the significance of a certain date, the authors in this anthology have taken this idea and run with it, writing stories to entertain and inspire. Even the format they were challenged to write within - a mini saga, a story told in just 100 words - shows that numeric influence is all around! With infinite numbers, there are infinite possibilities...

The result is a thrilling and absorbing collection of tales written in a variety of styles, and it's a testament to the creativity of these young authors.

Here at Young Writers it's our aim to inspire the next generation and instill in them a love of creative writing, and what better way than to see their work in print? The imagination and skill within these pages show just a fraction of the writing skill of the next generation, and it's proof that we might just be achieving that aim! Congratulations to each of these fantastic authors, they should be very proud of themselves.

CONTENTS

THE STORIES

I'm Introduced As 02140

I'm introduced as 02140. It's been like that for the past year. I know everyone's number because it's on everybody's necks and wrists. I wake up next to 02141 and we nod. If you try to talk they'll shush you discretely. You cannot talk, just think. Sometimes it feels like you can't do that. We walk to breakfast and don't wake up the Dijas. If you wake them, you'll disappear. We enter and approach the linen to see the food. I want bacon, that's number 3 today so I hold up 3 fingers. We're trapped with everything numbers. Help!

Millie Turton (12)
Baysgarth School, Barton-Upon-Humber

My Number

I was concealed in a dark cupboard. Running from my attacker. I didn't want to believe this was truly happening. I should've listened to my friends when they warned me. Everything I ever had began to slip and got stored at the deepest part of my brain. For now, this was a game that I had to try and win. He was skilled. He was intelligent. He was agile. I was the exact opposite. My fears and thoughts had merged into one massive overload of emotions. He was after my number. The luckiest and most powerful of all number 7.

Lillie-May Coupland (16)
Baysgarth School, Barton-Upon-Humber

The Race

"10, 9," the stopwatch was counting down. I had 10 seconds to prove I could do this. "8, 7." My feet trembling with pain but I had to carry on. The screams from the crowd drowned my ears. "6, 5." My opponent was getting close. I needed to push through. "4, 3." Suddenly my goal was in sight. The end was in sight. "2, 1." I could do this!
Then I felt it, the red ribbon on my stomach. It felt like glory so I took my place on the 1st podium. I did it with 1 second to spare.

Freya Seddon (12)
Baysgarth School, Barton-Upon-Humber

I Am 24

24... Everywhere. I can't escape it! I live in the 24th house of the 24th street in the 24th room. 24 items on every single shelf. Everything the 24th colour. It all just seems the same. The number 24 is imprinted on every piece of furniture and all of my clothes. I cannot escape my house. There are no doorknobs. Food shaped like a 24 appears every 24th hour in my 24 kitchen cabinets. The world starts spinning, the number 24 is warping around me. By now I'm encased, I see nothing. I wake up, I'm number 24...

Mia Holden (12)
Baysgarth School, Barton-Upon-Humber

Trapped In The Integer

13, 13. If he rolls one more he will be trapped in the Integer. The dice click and clank, 13... He blinks and everything is black and then he falls. Everything becomes code, it's all Os and Is. He's back in his room but it's code. The chair, the bed, the desk, all Os and Is but everything else is black. But then he comes, the man who caused it all. The Integer, also known as 13. He stood in front of him. He wasn't human. He wasn't anything, just Os and Is. He was 1101, binary code for 13...

Jacob Lacy (12)
Baysgarth School, Barton-Upon-Humber

21 Minutes

It was a blur. All sense of direction was lost. I don't remember much about that day, all I know is that bad things happened. I'll tell you what I remember. Me and the boys geared up. We pulled our balaclavas over our heads and got in the van. Duffle bags in hand. I sat and thought 21 minutes in poor, out rich, or at least that's what we planned. It didn't go that way did it though? We got in vault 21 until Bill tells me, "I'm sorry, it's the end of the line for you..."

Freddie Roberts (12)

Baysgarth School, Barton-Upon-Humber

Then There Was None

Then there was nothing, no buildings, no light and no people, nothing was left but me. One day earlier, I was perfecting my master plan, when I got this strange message: 'You don't know what you're doing'. I was confused. Why and who sent me this, but I just continued. 1 hour until I finally win. I put the pieces together, joy, success and power fill me as I connect the last piece. 1 minute until I rule the world. I put the item in place and set it off, blinded by what happened next.

Rochann Silcott (14) & Megan
Baysgarth School, Barton-Upon-Humber

10 Million

I was public enemy number 1... Sirens, all around me. 10 million from all that smoke... Amazing isn't it? My mask made me sweat, the guns on my chest were shot, I was burning up. I prayed to god... I woke up, number 10 buzzed into my watch. My cell opened. My shock shook me out of my bed. A booming voice came and put me in even more shock. I needed to get out of here! This is crazy, I hate this place! I've been here before and escaped but this is worse, much, much worse. For breakfast, slop.

Myles Smith (12)

Baysgarth School, Barton-Upon-Humber

Number 61

I wake up with the number 61 on my arm. I get up and I'm inside. I look around but there's nothing but 61 everywhere. I'm trapped! 61 rooms on each floor with 61 things, the same things. I'm let out of my cell and go outside and count the cars. 61 cars... I can't escape because there are 61 doors to get through to escape all with keylocks. There's a dice game from 1 to 100. I roll it and get a 61. I can't escape the number 61! I realise I am stuck here forever and ever!

Ethan Cook (12)
Baysgarth School, Barton-Upon-Humber

Room 13

Who was in room 13? Where are they now? I need to find them. I need to save them from this horrible world outside of their room. Whoever it is I will get them back in here. Once you enter you are not meant to leave so here I am about to go on the journey of a lifetime to make them return to their assigned room, number 13. Will I follow through on this journey or will I have to return empty-handed? I can't believe someone left, this has never happened before. However, it's come home...

Aaliyah Mullen (11)
Baysgarth School, Barton-Upon-Humber

143

It's 2099 and I wake up looking at a photo of me when I was young and my lover. A flashback had begun. It was 2023, I was 20 and on my way to save my love. But when I got there I was only confronted by a sign saying: *Complete Quiz*. I then saw another sign saying: *Name Song*. Suddenly, a song from Stray Kids played. '143, I Love You'. I straight away knew it. I typed in 143 on the keypad as there were only numbers. I did what I could do. I was released.

Laura Davies-Hollingsworth (12)
Baysgarth School, Barton-Upon-Humber

The Horror Of 13

We are the 13th winners but why us? Why me? This is how it started. I was taken to camp 13. To the bathroom. 13 kids in the room. A man spoke. "The game has begun, split into 3 groups, 1 killer, 3 groups. The game was called 13, at least the bath round. We survived. The only group of 4, 1 plus 3. The rest screamed, the rest died but why? Why? I question now. There are new kids, new rounds but I, but me, I am now the horror, the ruler, the feared. I am now the killer.

Isabelle Birch
Baysgarth School, Barton-Upon-Humber

The Curse

I woke up at 7 o'clock. I looked down at my iPhone 7. I got an unexpected call from 19838434 but realised the last number was 7. They called at 7 o'clock. I felt a pain in my spine. 7 times. *This is a coincidence.* I shook my head. 7 times again. I walked into the kitchen, 7 steps to make a cup of tea. 7 scoops of everything. *Have I been cursed?* All of a sudden, a voice spoke. I went stony-faced. "You have 7 minutes left..."

Lucie Wood (12)
Baysgarth School, Barton-Upon-Humber

The Murder

I rolled a 6... It was right. The snow was falling away. I seek house number 36. If I had blood on my face I'll have hundreds of eyes on me. I arrive at house 36. My mate called but I ignored him. A guy came out of house 36, I shot him. The snow dyed red. The family came out in deep breaths and they faint... Now I'm wanted for murder. I'm hiding, waiting for my next victim, number 7. I kidnapped number 7 in the bright of the day...

Theo Marshall (11)
Baysgarth School, Barton-Upon-Humber

Outcome 6

"Psst. Wake up."

"Huh?" I say. "Who are you?"

"Never mind that," says a man, "just listen to me. You must change your fate. Now hurry!"

He shoves me inside a purple portal into a room with a woman, who looks like me, working on an invention.

"Can you hear me?" The man's voice fills my ears. "Good. Now stop the car accident."

She leaves the house. Following her, she walks onto a crosswalk, a car is about to hit her. I realise we are in a spaceship.

"Outcome 6. Mission completed," I hear a Vocaloid say.

Milena Ntin (12)
Christ Church CE Secondary Academy, Yardley Wood

Room Number 7

Silence. She had to be quiet. She stretched her hand out to rub the door. *Room number 7*, she thought. It was calling her. She opened the door, hit with the revolting scent of rot, she immediately held her nose. "Yuck," she gestured, acting like she was throwing up. She walked forward. Every shaking step made a little creaky noise. Spiderwebs were brushing against her face and the smell was getting stronger every step she took. Suddenly, she stopped. There was a large, wooden wardrobe. She felt her hand open the door, and 7 rotting bodies of children fell out.

Scarlett Skinley (11)

Christ Church CE Secondary Academy, Yardley Wood

The End

It was 2099. I was the last one, or so I thought in the bleak sickening hospital. A chemical aroma lingered in the air. What was it? I cleaned the corpses yesterday. Anyway, I heard footsteps. It wasn't me! *Tip-tap,* it repeated. Getting closer and closer. My heart started pounding faster and faster like a cheetah. I shot up out of bed. The thin white sheets crinkled and my hospital gown slid down my shoulder. I dived out of the fire exit. A cold, bitter hand lay on my sweaty shoulder. I froze, my body shook. "Come here, my child."

Lily Dowding (11)

Christ Church CE Secondary Academy, Yardley Wood

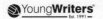

0700-85969 - The Challenge

Day 1. The call. 0700-85968... I picked up. "Hello. You have been chosen to participate in a challenge! Your number is 8. Press 1 if you accept."
I put down the phone as I knew it was a scam call.
Day 2 was the same, except the number was 0700-85969 and I was 9. I noticed the pattern. I pressed 1. I was teleported to a cell. On the wall was '0700-85969: 9. Find the pattern'. I knew what it was. "The last number in 0700-85969 is nine and I'm 9." A door opened... I proceeded to the next cell...

Mia Wilkes (11)
Christ Church CE Secondary Academy, Yardley Wood

Happy Hotels

Me, my sister and my dad headed out of the car, it was a long hour but here we are. The woman behind the desk was wearing baggy overalls, her hair was in a mess of a bun, a cigarette was half-lit in her mouth. "Welcome to Happy Hotels," she began. "Your number is 128. Have a lovely day." She spoke like she hadn't had a night's rest in forever. As we walked up a smell of smoke lingered around the hall.
"Okay, here we are, room 128," pronounced Dad. As my sister and I looked we were horrified.

Chloe Lees (11)
Christ Church CE Secondary Academy, Yardley Wood

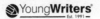

20 Ruined It All...

20... I am officially 20 and everything changes here. No more going to school, having it all easy. No more hugs from Mum every night. All because of an age number. 20. I could wail on the spot, exactly 20 hot moist tears dripping down my oily face. This was terrible. My biggest fear was happening. The boxes were all packed up neatly in rows. 20 boxes. There seemed to be so many things including the number 20. It gave me a migraine just thinking about it. I guess it's happening. Their waves are just turning into little blurs.

Hannah Poozesh (12)

Christ Church CE Secondary Academy, Yardley Wood

666

Never answer a call that ends in 666. That's what they all told me day after day, month after month, but however many times I was told I just wouldn't listen. Friday the 13th. The worst day of my life. My phone rang, I checked the ending digits. 666. Me, being the naive person that I am, I answered the call. There wasn't a voice on the other end just a high-pitched ringing. It got louder and louder. My phone cracked. My heart stopped beating. I took one final breath. It all went dark. 666 is my greatest enemy.

Samantha Cunningham-Elsby (11)
Christ Church CE Secondary Academy, Yardley Wood

99, Who I Am Now

Sitting next to me, I saw number 98. Every year the orphanage takes in 100 new orphans. My parents died 7 months ago, so I'm surprised they've taken this long to take me in. I miss my parents, but the shock has died down now. My brother went missing two months ago too. The boy next to me looks at my tag. "99?" he asks. "Who's 100?" Then suddenly, the van jolts to a stop, before an enormous grey, boring building. It looms over us as we walk towards it. This is my new home now...

Eleanor Vaughan (11)

Christ Church CE Secondary Academy, Yardley Wood

In Exactly 4 Seconds

My favourite number is 4. Everything in my life is based around the number 4. There were 4 people in my family, I had 4 friends in school. My door number was 4 and I was born on 4/4/2004. This didn't mean much to my family but I knew it had a special meaning. We are now in 2048. I'm 44 years old. There are 4 people in my family. My door number is 4. I have 4 main friends and I was born on 4/4/2004. Today is my birthday and in exactly 4 seconds my life will change forever...

Anna Todor (12)
Christ Church CE Secondary Academy, Yardley Wood

Only 30 Seconds Left

Only 30 seconds left. I walked out of my room at 12:30. I had 30 seconds left. I didn't know what to do so I said goodbye to my family and friends. I then realised that I don't have 30 seconds left, I have 20 seconds. I then saw all of my friends and said goodbye. I had 10 seconds left. I went to sleep for 3 seconds and I had 7 seconds left and I hugged all of my family. I had 5 seconds left. I spent those 5 seconds crying...

Maisie Dixon (12)
Christ Church CE Secondary Academy, Yardley Wood

The Remaining

The population was rapidly increasing and food around the world was being eaten faster than we populate. That's until Project 2 Billion came into place, the disease spread faster than I'd ever seen, with zombies everywhere. The plan went wrong, the government lost control of the disease. All cities are remote and covered by plants and nature, zombies ruled the world, it was over for us, over for me. Shops I raided were out of supplies and I can't do anything about it. I was one of the remaining but now I'm going to be one of the lost.

Ellie Murray (14)
St Joseph's College, Dumfries

5 Minutes Left

"5 minutes left," NASA explains, as a colossal meteor strikes through the atmosphere.
"Is there time for evacuation?" asks the president sternly.
"I'm afraid that's not possible, sir!" says the assistant. A long period of silence happens. Finally, the assistant says, "Well, there is one spark of hope. There is a boy, Sir, rumours spread that he has powers!"
"Is he our last hope?" says the president.
"I am afraid so, Sir, he is our last hope..."
"Call his parents right away!" says the president.
"Yes, Sir!" says the assistant. "You Sir, have made the right choice..."

Ayaan Ahmed (12)
Stopsley High School, Luton

Agent 00

Beep... "Agent 00 to the Master, immediately." My heart's pacing. I'm in grave danger.
"Good evening Agent, it's been some time, I have a task for you."
The master is the controller of us. He has a remote explosive chip inside our brains, he can detonate at any time. He kills debtors, we've no choice but to obey.
"What is it?" I stutter.
"I need you to... kill... your mother."
"Please! No! Why?" But I already know the answer. I grab the gun and arrive at my mother's house. The door opens.
"Sweetie, what are you doing here?"
Bang!

Jason Kalosi (14)
Stopsley High School, Luton

The Double Hour

It was the year 2222, at 22:02, a girl named Cherry lay wide awake staring into the darkness, waiting... Suddenly, out from the shadows appeared what she had been waiting for.
"You wanted to see us Agent Blossom?"
"Indeed, we need to discuss Double Hour!" Cherry Blossom replied. "Before it's too late."
"We need to take action, we have 20 minutes," exclaimed the 22nd agent.
"Ready the force fields, it's coming," Cherry instructed.
That night, at 22:22, the Double Hour came through a magic portal bringing 222 monsters. It was time, time for Double Hour!

Bethany Turnstill (11)
Stopsley High School, Luton

2pm

I wake up to cats barking, my head pounding, my back aching, that's normal around here. I sit up and look around my dark, empty room. Maya runs in. "Why aren't you up, Milly?" Maya asks.
"Time?" I ask.
"2pm," she replies.
"20 minutes left, sis," Maya says while rolling her eyes.
I slowly get up, grab a jacket and open my window.
"Well, come on then," I yell.
Maya runs over, we climb through my window. It's dark outside, all the trees are dead, the floor is mud. I look around. "It's gone... We are too late..." I say.

Mia Larsen (12)
Stopsley High School, Luton

21 Minutes

21 minutes left. Once upon a time, there were 2 people in a house. Their names were Max and Patricia. They were on their phones. At 21:00 Max shouted out, "OMG!"
Patricia said, "What?"
"We only have 21 minutes left to live," said Max.
"What should we do?" Patricia asked.
"Let's go explore," Max said.
"Okay," Patricia said.
They left the house and they saw the woods. They went into the woods and started exploring. They saw a house on top of the hill and they started climbing up the hill to knock on the door. They knocked...

Alfie Devane (11)
Stopsley High School, Luton

2%

2%, I have 2%. I'm lost with 2%. It's dark, no street lights. Keep running. Just keep running. Get home. Mum will be mad. Keep going. No. Stop. What's that? He's coming... Crack in pavement. Stumble, catch breath. Must keep going. Faster. Turn corner. What street is this? Wait. No. Not enough time to stop. Listen. Footsteps. Speeding up. Don't look back. Please. He's talking. Don't listen. Keep going. It was all fine. What's gonna happen? He's getting faster and louder. Faster. Breathe. In. Out. Speed up. Where am I? I don't know. He's coming. Stop. One second. No. 1%...

Jenny Doherty (13)
Stopsley High School, Luton

The Unlucky 5

5.5.1995. 5 curious children, Hannah, Daniel, Lewis, Eliana and Adam were walking home when they passed a haunted house. "We should visit," said Hannah.
"How about tomorrow?" said Lewis.
"Yes!" everyone shouted.
The next day, they all met up outside 'Haunted Reality House' on Bloods Point Drive. After a while, they heard something. Next thing they knew Adam and Hannah went missing. The 3 others got scared and went outside to call the police. Just as they were heading out the lights went out. When Daniel got back out Lewis and Eliana had disappeared...

Aisha Bawor (12)
Stopsley High School, Luton

Visor 1.0

In a white, shimmering laboratory, microscopes and machines, wires were attached to a glass container large enough to fit a man. Suddenly, a voice from a speaker said, "Open container 1.0." A robot emerged from its container. Blue lights came from its forehead. Its body was white with blue lights. The robot's name was Visor 1.0, or 1.0 for short. 1.0's programming was to save E-1 (formerly known as Earth) from infection. The probe hopped into a spaceship. 3... 2... 1... Launch! The spaceship shot off into distant space. In the distance, infected E-1 came closer to the robot's view.

Abbas Agha (11)
Stopsley High School, Luton

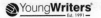

A Dangerous Gamble

Only 30 seconds left. I needed to crack the code, I needed to... otherwise... There is no time. Another bad code. *Thud. Thud.* Daunting footsteps loomed closer to me. Maybe 300300. No. I'm nervous, anxious. No time, I must carry on. I must... *Knock, knock.* My thoughts were interrupted by 30 ominous knocks on number 30, floor 2. 10 seconds left. My instinct told me to run but I froze. Vibrations! I felt vibrations in the floor. Head pounding, heart racing, door beeping... The door was beeping. "Oh no! Run!" I shouted.
Then they replied with, "Or else pretty..."

Amelia Deller (11)
Stopsley High School, Luton

Population Overload

It's been 30 years... I'm subject 121C and I was frozen 30 years ago to stop overpopulation and world starvation. Scientists are working on time machines to send humans to the past, to 2293 or something. It's 2399 if you're wondering. Some psychopaths are killing people and turning them into robots. Some countries don't face this problem yet, they are currently dealing with a deadly purge. Schools are no longer in business so we need to take these 'knowledge pills'. Buildings are collapsing, society is slowly losing sanity. It will all end soon. The purge has begun...

Iona Norton (11)
Stopsley High School, Luton

The Last Day

Tuesday 31st October, 1985, Bella and Ruby were cuddling on the couch watching a horror movie. It was dark and humid outside and a cold breeze filled the room. Suddenly, there was a noise and Bella disappeared. She found a mysterious room and found out the truth. A crackly voice appeared. *Boom!* Ruby ran into the room. "Bella's dead," screamed Ruby. The police came and comforted Ruby. She told them what happened and they were surprised but they thought it wasn't Ruby. They found nothing around the house and left. Ruby stopped crying and slowly she started smiling.

Emilia Niemiec (11)
Stopsley High School, Luton

20, Number 20

20 on my shorts, 20 on the back of my shirt. 2-2 versus Sacred Heart, the best team in the league. Flashbacks from our last meeting. 7-0 defeat. That was the cup, this is the league. We grab this game and Division 1 here I come. Harry skillfully drags back into a quick counter. *Pass it, man, play me!* begging in my head. Of course, my telepathic midfielder plays me an excellent through ball. I accelerate away and give it to Jiriyah. *You've gotta square, don't shoot!* Expectedly he did, smashed wide. Gotta go again, not again, this can't happen again...

Israel Igoche (13)
Stopsley High School, Luton

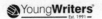

A Boy With A Dream

It was 2045. Filipos was just a boy with an ambitious dream. Playing football. It had been since day 1. He was now 14. But WW3 had begun. Footballer or fighter? That was the question. Ma said, "Fighter!" Unfortunately, that was the only answer. 14, he lied. Now 18, fighting for his life. *Bang!* He collapsed. He couldn't feel anything. Filipos woke up confused. Miracles happen. This was another example. 2080, the year he was in a wheelchair, having lived to see the city revived from its war state, thanks to his donations. Aged 49, just a man, with pride.

Fraser Huntly (12)
Stopsley High School, Luton

Fantasy 5

Fantasy 5 was a group of 5 people who survived the zombie outbreak. It all started when scientists in China experimented on trying to bring the dead back to life. The experiment went wrong and an oozing liquid erupted and flooded the whole room. Then, it happened! Green and disfigured people started running at others screaming for food. The scientists had no chance. Everyone was dead. Hours later, the story was everywhere around the world and people were panicking. The human race would eventually have to end and today would be the day unless 5 strong people stopped it.

Adrian Mihail Florea (12)
Stopsley High School, Luton

The Statue

"Get out of the cell." I couldn't argue, they both had guns. As I walked down the hallways, I saw 2 other people in orange jumpsuits. Eventually, we got to a large door with an unreadable sign. Then the comms went off. "Maintain eye contact and don't blink." The heavy metal door slid open revealing a statue in the corner.

"Don't blink," I repeated to myself... until... I blinked... It moved, I heard shots, screams and bones snapping. I saw the 2 others fall. I ran, but not fast enough... He got me... 173 was his name... 173...

Allan Ochendal (12)
Stopsley High School, Luton

The Last 106 Metres Left

I'm number 106 in the Fish Games still aiming to win. Hunger, anger, sadness, a fusion of emotions emerge throughout the tournament. Today is the last game, it's a race. Today's challenge is heart-racing. I am given a Lamborghini and a helmet. They tell me and 5 others to race. It starts at 1:06pm. Nerves increasing, hearts pounding as 1 minute remains on the clock. It starts, speed and handling determine the race. 15th gear, 2nd gear, 3rd gear. I'm drifting past Sainsbury's with 106 metres left to win it. Emotions freeze as I pass the chequered flag.

Ayaan Tanvir (12)
Stopsley High School, Luton

The Mission

"How'd it go?" said the general.
"Job's finished, chief," answered the lieutenant.
The lieutenant was tasked with holding down an important building with part of his squad. The building was crucial to winning the war.
"The war documents are safe and in our hands, right?" asked the general.
"They abandoned me and joined the Shadow Squad, it was just me," replied the lieutenant.
"You held the building all by yourself! How many were there?" asked the general hurriedly.
"237."

Jakub Niemiec (13)
Stopsley High School, Luton

AI, The Matrix, The World And The Universe

Life is a number... All our intelligence lies within numbers, especially 0 and 1. Binary code is found in everything, in the words you read right now. 01100010 could mean anything and so could 1110001001. This is a concept used to create AI, The Matrix, the world. And the universe. It is something you'll probably never notice because it lies behind the reality you have been taught, everything you know; and it terrifies me. Yet the more you think about it, the further it extends, because you can go infinitely, just like AI, The Matrix, the world. And the universe...

Kacper Szymczakowski (12)
Stopsley High School, Luton

Whatever You Do, Don't Look Back

I was standing outside room 666, where they told me to go with one tip: "Whatever you do, don't look back."
With deep breaths and shaking legs, I stepped in, with only one thing in my head - don't look back. After all, 666 was a devil's number.
There was a long hallway, almost endless. After a while, I felt someone following me... but I wasn't supposed to look back. I heard screams coming from the direction I was going. The only mistake I made was looking back.
Now I'm stuck in room 666, waiting for the next person to come.

Minahal Waheed (12)
Stopsley High School, Luton

Down On One Knee

I stepped up to the door, the number '11' sitting above the window, tapping it lightly, double checking the flowers I got her. Then there she was, wearing her lovely magenta dress, the decorative gems shimmering in the moonlight. We walked toward the restaurant as I handed her the flowers. Once we had arrived at the restaurant, we went outside and she sat down, the highly decorated area making it perfect for the surprise. The waiter lit the tall candles on the table, leaving right after. I pulled out the black box from my pocket, getting down on one knee...

Anaya Purdue (11)
Stopsley High School, Luton

The Haunted House

I was down to my last £19. A man offered to rent me a room. The man was sketchy. He said the house was haunted but I said, "I'll take it."
When I got there, there was this woman waiting for me. She said, "Welcome."
I said, "Hi!"
She replied, "Hey."
She asked for my name and I replied, "Connie." I then asked for her name and she suddenly disappeared. I wondered what to do. "Wait, is that her?" I shouted. "Wait, no!" as the curtain fell. "I'm scared."

Connie-Mae Smith (11)
Stopsley High School, Luton

Gone

Only 30 seconds left till he will approach. I begin to bite my tongue out of stress. *Creak!* I hear footsteps getting closer and closer. The door begins to turn. My stomach starts to feel like it's twisting. A tall man walks in. I can slightly see his face. Sweat is dripping down my forehead. *Ring, ring.* The man's phone goes. The voice says, "She's gone." I realise the voice is my mother. This is my chance to escape.
"Mum!" I scream.
"I'm coming to save you, only 30 seconds, 30 seconds..."

Hailey Masuka (11)
Stopsley High School, Luton

Butterflies

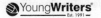

98, 99,100! They just keep appearing. It's weird, there are never any butterflies in these fields, so why are there so many now? They're all the same type too, how strange. The blue morpho. They can't survive in these conditions. They can't be here. One of them landed on me. Then another. Then another. Soon enough all I saw was black and blue. A sharp pain shot across my whole body in a flash. That's when I realised what was happening. I accepted it, it's a weird feeling to have your blood drained by hundreds of mini straw-like tongues.

Keira Duffy (14)
Stopsley High School, Luton

Demonic Trap

I peer through my fingers. My heart's pounding. Only 30 seconds left. The clock is racing as if it's running a marathon. I gulp. My throat's arid like the baguettes in our school canteen. I can feel my tears drop but it isn't sadness, it's the pressure. The hassle. I have to decide. Fast. One more step onto the surface and I will be lost in the concluded, unknown darkness. I am getting carried away by the hysteria. One more step and the luminous monster is approaching towards me, set to devour me undividedly. Demon trap... They are here...

Tahsiath Bintee Alam Tanmi (12)
Stopsley High School, Luton

The March

Only 30 minutes left. I was passionate about this mission. I could finally be promoted to captain. I can't mess this up. *Boom!* What? The attack wasn't meant to start yet. "Gear up!" I shouted into the radio. An armada of blue, ornate parachutes dotted in the sky glided down from the bombarded and ambushed jets. I slammed the button and the floor opened up. We met the recruits venturing across the barren land. The rest of air support mixed their speed and sacrificed themselves to open the towering metal gates. We marched straight in.

Yuvraj Lali (11)
Stopsley High School, Luton

Earth To Mars

It's 3022 and chaos is everywhere. Earth has litter located anywhere you go. Gas has filled the air and we never see the sun anymore. Scientists say they're doing everything they can, but I don't believe them. On a rocket, they flew us to Mars. They put a dome around Mars and put oxygen inside. Food, water, animals were sent to Mars. There was a water shortage and everyone was panicking. It was a disaster. All we could think of was water. Our mouths were starting to dry. Using chemicals they managed to create water, but everything was different.

Sumaiya Rahman (11)
Stopsley High School, Luton

Mission: Save The Earth

I was public enemy number one. I still am. Just about to plant a bomb to destroy Earth at my house. People start noticing, screaming, running around. Officer 0.5 enters my house number 434.56. He knows something strange is going on, the glass shatters, the earth shakes. Quickly, I escape the house before he finds me. Sudden destruction is imminent. Only 30 seconds left. 2 wires, which one to pick? Will he pick life or death? Quickly, he picks the green wire. Has he done it, has he saved Earth from the destruction caused by me...? The clock is ticking...

William Chambers (12)

Stopsley High School, Luton

Last Word

I opened my eyes slowly and found myself in a hospital bed. I was so confused as I looked around. I saw doctors around me. "Why am I here?" I asked.
"You are here to have surgery. If the operation doesn't work, you won't make it."
I gulped as I heard the news. Later on the doctors did the surgery, but... something was wrong. My heart was slowing down. The doctors got worried and tried everything to save me but... it was too late... I only had 20 seconds to say my last words. My last word was, "Goodbye..."

Rebecca Derby (12)
Stopsley High School, Luton

My End

It's my turn, I need to roll at least 5. But if I don't, the end. 5 days ago I 'borrowed' money from a very powerful man, but he isn't persuaded about asking me why. Here I go... With luck... I threw the dice, my eyes were glued together... A 4... I lost. My body died for 5 seconds. Walking away everything I thought about was the 5 hours till they find me. *Run... run...* that's my thoughts... while going home. There I suddenly hear someone knocking loudly at the door 5 times. "Is this how I'm going to die?"

Ivett Boldizsar (13)
Stopsley High School, Luton

13

13, the most satanic number you can think of. And I'm born with it. It's engraved in me. Stuck with me. 13 used to be my favourite number until my husband went missing on Friday 13th November 2013. Ever since I've been getting missed calls every day. Same number... 0479781***. 13 knocks, only at the 13th of each month at 13:13. I came home today... 13 red pencils scattered on the floor. 13 red gumdrops leading to the bathroom. I saw blood. Opened the shower curtains. There he was, dead. Surrounded by blood with the number 13 written on him.

Mehrab Khan (13)
Stopsley High School, Luton

Sweet 16

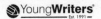

16, 16, all I could think of was my Sweet 16. I woke up with a dash of energy running all around. "Mum?" I asked. "Dad?" Nothing. I opened a window for a breeze, instead, got a fright. The world was crumbling before my eyes. My death, my fate, coming towards me faster than I could participate. The Grim Reaper, ready to snatch my soul. I tried running out through the front, no luck. Devoured. I jumped out the back window looking for help, a reason. *Poof!* It went pitch-black... It was my Sweet 16. It was all repeating again.

Atif Ahmed (11)
Stopsley High School, Luton

Scary Science

2022, there was something cruel in the city, a terrifying science experiment that took place in an isolated part of the city. It was far in the mountains. Sadly everything ended badly for AbrahamJoe 11. He was the one who took part in the freezing experiment.
2069, AbrahamJoe 11 woke up in pain. He looked around and everything was demolished. He decided to scream for help but there was no answer. Suddenly, he heard scrunching from the back. He got really curious about what it was. With all his power he stood up. He was shocked by what he saw...

Gabriel Giiszczynski (13)
Stopsley High School, Luton

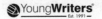

What If It Didn't Happen?

Slowly awakening from my restless and dreamless slumber, the slumber that I didn't remember entering, I tried to rise, but I realised... my hands were drenched in a crimson liquid. It was blood... The number 27 had been repeatedly carved into my arm. I stared at my arm in horror as I tried to recall how it got there.
Clang!
A jagged piece of razor-sharp glass slipped out of my numb hand and shattered on the ground. I couldn't have... could I? What felt like 1,000 hands reached out from behind and firmly grasped my back...

Inayah Shah (12)
Stopsley High School, Luton

1918

It was 1918 in Normandy, France. *Boom!* Gunshots were fired as Tom quickly took cover and avoided death. It was snowing in France as it was January. Tom had met this man called Gregoravich. He was Russian. Tom only had one bullet left and he shot Gregoravich. He knew that Gregoravich was a Russian spy. He had come here from Moscow and was trying to get information. Just as that happened, a loud bang was heard and the bullet came straight at Tom. He lay there motionless while a lagoon of blood spurted out. Gregoravich is still alive today.

Noah Knapper (12)
Stopsley High School, Luton

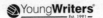

Only A Day To Go

It's only 1 day left till I (Dixie) can leave this hell of a hotel, it's terrifying. "Baby, breakfast is ready," my mum yelled but I'm not even hungry. *Sigh...* When I get home I will sit on my bed and watch some nice relaxing TV. When I'm here I hear whispers of some name, 'Harley', but I don't get why it will only talk to me not my mum (Charly) and my dad (Jason) and they can't hear it either. It's so stressful. I'm not lying and I always wonder, *why does it have to be me...?*

Ebony Maddams (11)
Stopsley High School, Luton

Bye-Bye Annie Fisher

370. Locked. 371. Locked. 372, unlocked! "This is it, no going back from here." *Creak!* The door was opened. Mr Fisher looked around for anything that could be his daughters. He looked around until he found something. "Argh!" Mr Fisher screamed. His daughter's body was tied to a chair. She was covered in cuts and bruises. She was dead. In the blink of an eye, her body vanished and a glow of light appeared outside of the window. He ran down the stairs to the front of the building and what he saw was horrifying...

Summer Smith (11)
Stopsley High School, Luton

A Wave Of Indecision

30 seconds, that's all it is. Nothing more, nothing less. Every nanosecond of life built up to this moment. My hands become clammy, every finger pattern clasped deeply around every groove on the patterns of the ball. Is this the feeling of the zone? I brought the ball down and followed it through aiming for the basket, as the ball left my hand, I felt a rush. 2 seconds remaining. The ball was circling around the hoop. A wave of indecisiveness flowed through my body and that was it. Everything went black. It's all over now. I have lost.

Michael Kiboro (13)
Stopsley High School, Luton

The Final

I am number 9. It's coming down to the last 5 minutes and neither team has scored (yet). I receive the ball from my teammate and drive forward. I dance my way through the midfielders showing all my skills, by turning and twisting my way through. I then pass the first defender by slipping the ball through her legs, nutmeg! The crowd roars loving my energy. I take the ball a touch to the right and *bam!* I watch my shot rocket past the goalkeeper into the net. "Goal! Yes! We won the final," my teammates shout, piling on me.

Maya Chowdhoury (12)
Stopsley High School, Luton

Kate, My Lucky Number 8

I see apartment number 8. That's my lucky and favourite number and Kate's my favourite person. She's my lucky number personified, the number more lucky. She's stunning, pleasant, cheerful. The only 4 letter word for her is love. Our 4 letter names merge to 8, a symbol of infinity. But now I'm gone, my heart torn in 2, my lucky number with it. Now they're no more. My 8 letter words to describe her crack to 4. Now the only word I can use is fate, what she's truly supposed to be. My lovely Kate, turned to be my fate.

Verity McTigue (13)
Stopsley High School, Luton

3 To Go?

It was 12 o'clock, Friday the 26th of November. I thought to myself, *3 hours.* You may ask till what? The hours flew by and by. It was 30 seconds to go. Everyone was trying not to let out a cheer but, "Yeah!" screamed the whole school ready to leave. Freddie, Ali, John, Noah and Antonio all let out a few screams.

"Weekend," screamed Year 7.

After it had all calmed down all the teachers prepared to leave. 6 minutes later, the teachers left. 10 minutes later no one was left. All 17 hallways are empty.

Freddie Botham (11)
Stopsley High School, Luton

The Rocket Ship That Disappeared

Sam climbed aboard the space rocketship on 1/1/1111. He was going to space to find a new planet for people to live on. "1 minute until take-off. 60, 59, 58."
"Wait, what?" The rocket started and climbed over 4,000mph, the rocket is taking off. The rocket just disappeared. "Wait, what?" The sky is red, the ground is destroyed. Sam opened his eyes. He couldn't believe it. The sky is pink and the clouds are green. The ground was made up of broken buildings, rubbish and floating in the air he saw a dragon.

Jacob Walsh (13)
Stopsley High School, Luton

The Unknown Caller

It was dark and gloomy... Lights flickered in the distance of the corridor. My heart thumping was the only noise I was able to hear. I slowly walked into a classroom to find a number written in blood on the wall. 0787663****. My phone rang. It was from the number, I struggled to answer because of my shaky hands. I finally answered and blood-curdling screams came from the phone. "Amy, wake up!" I'd had a nightmare again. I noticed something on my leg. I squinted to try and read it. It was the same phone number. My eyes widened.

Amy Booth (13)
Stopsley High School, Luton

30

30 seconds left. My heart was racing. I frantically looked around for something. A clue, a hint, anything. 15 seconds. I looked up, my eyes darting around the room. Tears blurred my vision. I don't know where I am, who I am. I just woke up here. In an empty room. On my own. No instruction, no introductions, wearing a dark blue jumpsuit with '30' tattooed onto my wrist. 5. Oh god. 4. A feeling of panic washed over me. No, please no... 3. What's happening? 2. No... The last thing I remember is a massive, white blinding flash.

Madelaine Keeling (13)
Stopsley High School, Luton

The Phone

On the 22nd August every year, the same number rings, 789789789. If you answer what you hear is, "I'm in your house," then the sound of a window breaking. But one year the phone rang and the voice answered as usual but I hadn't touched the phone. Then an ear-piercing scream. One night on the 21st August I remembered what happened last year when it called but it said goodbye. Rex, my dog, I was hugging him but it was just his dead body. Never trust the phone. It plays tricks on you. Trust me before it gets you too...

Honey Hopewell (11)
Stopsley High School, Luton

Lucky 3

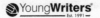

3 was the number I was given by my head coach. It was the number I wore proudly on the back of my T-shirt, as I stepped into the football stadium for the 3rd time. However, this was no ordinary stadium, it was one of the most populated stadiums of all time. It was the World Cup Stadium. I was standing inside for the 3rd and final time. Something odd was happening though. There were only 3 fans. It was 3 o'clock and kick-off should have started 3 minutes ago. The opposition wasn't pitch-side. I've feared this day would come...

Ellis Freckleton (14)
Stopsley High School, Luton

Opposites

Theo and Sianna have always hated each other since Year 2. Sianna is an A* student. Theo's grades are dropping and his behaviour is getting worse. When their maths teacher asks Sianna to help Theo she wants to say no but her teacher brought the fact she knew Sianna's family was struggling so her teacher offered to pay the fee for the college she wants to go too. Sianna agreed; she really needed the money. They studied with each other for 2 months and finally she has the guts to ask him the question she's been dying to know...

Elissa Mziu (13)
Stopsley High School, Luton

One Day, I Hope...

My favourite number is 4. Some people think it's unusual,
but it's on my kit. It gives me confidence. Like in the last few
games I saved the last 4 goals. Hopefully one day, I'll make
it to the World Cup and get 7 Ballon d'Ors, just like Messi.
Number 10 he was, but now he's 30.
January 4th, my mum said, "Dream big and you may
achieve."
So ever since, I've dreamed big and worked harder than I
ever did before. I joined a team, then joined the academy.
Soon I may become a pro with many medals.

Saffa Syeda Islam (12)
Stopsley High School, Luton

Doors

The lift opened on floor 111. They stepped out. Bob saw a locked door. Everyone looked for a key. Nigel found the key and unlocked the door. There was a long hallway. They opened door 2. Door 3 was switching places but they got through. Door 4 was surrounded by iron bars. They found a lever which opened the gate. They heard a scream. Leo and Bob hid in a wardrobe but the other 2 were killed. They kept on opening doors, hiding from monsters and solving puzzles. They opened drawers with food and water, the place was never-ending doors.

Leonis Lika
Stopsley High School, Luton

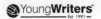

The Deep Death

I was outside the door. 237, that was the door number they told me to go to. I knocked but there was no answer. I knocked again. "Hello, anyone there? I'm from the police department." Still no answer. I started getting annoyed. I tried the handle, it opened. "It's so dark in here." I looked for the light switch. I found it, but when I turned around I saw something horrifying. 2 people split in half with all their teeth taken out. Then I heard a whisper right behind me saying, "You're next..."

Seth Allum (12)
Stopsley High School, Luton

The Times In 2089

011, was a lonely girl with no friends but had a power nobody else had. Her power was telekinesis. For now, it wasn't a usual power to have so was not practised much and she didn't know how to use it. Finally... it was 2089 when she was experimented on and she tried to escape multiple times but failed. Her powers were taken away because she caused harm to lots of people. But one day at the mysterious lab something happened... Her powers... they came back. She was more powerful than she ever was... Beware of the new demon...

Sonia Cacuci (11)
Stopsley High School, Luton

The Special One

Every soldier in the world has a number, it decides what powers you get. My friend got 57191, but I got 34... For some reason, everyone was shocked. No one has ever gotten it. The whistle was blown and the games had begun. The challenge was intense, we had to display our powers. 57191 passed as well as 6978. It was my turn. I was stressed but I went for it. I used my 34 powers. *Pow!* The whole world was destroyed in one blow! The judges were shocked, nothing like this had ever happened. "And the winner is... 34!"

Mohit Magesan (12)
Stopsley High School, Luton

2 Chimes

My phone chimed 2 times. A message? I stood there by the bar at the famous nightclub run by a masked DJ. My hips swayed to the escalating tempo of the music. The flow of music understands me, engulfs me, consumes me. The music changes abruptly. I scan the faces around me; they don't seem to mind. I search for the music source. My gaze meets the DJ's eyes. Body rigid, he reaches for his phone. I feel another set of chimes against my hand. Unnoticed by the crowd he reveals his face. I look at my phone. 'Remember me?'

Lidia Kruk (14)
Stopsley High School, Luton

The Untouched Clock

1 thousand... 1 thousand plus 1... I tossed my head back, letting a bitter laugh escape my mouth. My knees buckled. I felt my weak body fall to the plush white floor. I pulled myself back into a comfortable position to watch the clock. Always just out of reach. 1 thousand plus 2... Forever ticking. Darkness blurred the edge of my vision. The familiar taste of metal filled my mouth. I wiped at my cracked lips. I pulled my hand back to see a crimson stain dripping down my fingers. Everything collapsed in on me. 1 thousand plus 3...

Anya Shrosbree (13)
Stopsley High School, Luton

Mr Robin

Only 30 seconds left until my death. Someone had escaped and was killing everyone around them. I had a suspicion that something was wrong. Why was everyone acting normal when we could all be murdered? There was someone staring at me from across room 206. Looking bloodthirsty was my teacher, Mr Robin. He was the academy's maths teacher. I always thought he seemed strange. I was right, I knew when Mr Robin stabbed my heart out at 9:47 on the 7th December 2006. Somehow, I Jess Volf, was still alive and was coming for Mr Robin...

Remy Ward-Lindsay (11)
Stopsley High School, Luton

The 9 Curses

There was a man named Jonathan and one day when he was walking down the road he saw a machine with 9 numbers on it. Not thinking much of it Jonathan put in the £1 and the game said, "Choose a number 1-9." Jonathan chose 4.
"But what he doesn't know is that the numbers are all curses and each number gets worse," the man across the street said in dodgy ripped-up clothes. Not thinking anything of it he went to bed but when he got up his legs were paralysed for 4 hours and people were bullying him.

Finley Williams (13)
Stopsley High School, Luton

The Saviour

9 minutes of peace until it happened. Swimming peacefully nobody there. I heard something. I turned around, nothing. I heard the sound again. I turned around but this time there was someone with a knife! I swam and went underwater to get away. I couldn't breathe. I tried to get to the surface but there was no way out. I swam far away. I let go of holding my breath but realised I was underwater. I swam up and screamed using my last breath. "Help!" It was black. I saw nothing but I woke up being saved by a fisherman.

Bobby Robertson (11)
Stopsley High School, Luton

3...

I arrive in London. Strolling in Trafalgar Square I overhear a conversation between 2 policemen. They're talking about a missing person who goes by the name 3. Being the detective I am, I ask about it. They say it is none of my business. Of course, they say that. I walk into my apartment, apartment number 3, it has to be a coincidence. I just have to figure out why. I'll figure it out tomorrow. It's now Monday, I go to the coffee shop. I ask for a latte. When it arrives there's a 3 on it. I sip. *Thud...*

Lily Smith (12)
Stopsley High School, Luton

Time Was Ticking

The time was 3:15. I only have 15 minutes left. There was no possible code, I tried everything. What else could it be? I was breaking down at this point. Only 3:15, it kept repeating 3:15, 3:15. I guess this is it unless I try one more. *Beep, beep, beep.* "Sorry, incorrect pin," the machine said. I could only hear myself and the clock. The timer went off. Next, you know. *Bang!* I'm dead. Only 15 minutes left all because I wanted to be cool. This is all my fault. Now I am dead and no one stopped me.

Hafsa Jurevica (12)
Stopsley High School, Luton

Haunted 13

It was Friday 13th, 6am. I turn on the news, there was nothing interesting only some things about rare animals. 7am. I always have bad luck on the 13th but this time it is stronger, I nearly stabbed myself while making breakfast! 13:00, I turned on the news again after I showered. The reporter said that there were 13 murders scattered around the woods. The killer was unknown. The number 13 has haunted me since I was 12. I am not myself today. I was in the wood before the murders happened. My hands are stained red. It was me!

Marika Zielonka (12)
Stopsley High School, Luton

The Chair

5am. Why is time going by so slowly? I want this to be over. Hurry up... The palms of my hands get sweatier. I wipe my hands on my bedsheets. I stare at the clock on the white, tiled walls. 5:05am. Hurry up. I see my reflection in the mirror. They are watching me. I read the letters my daughter had sent me. Tears run down my cheeks. I bury my face in my hands. 5:07am. 3 minutes. The speakers go off, "3 minutes." I know. Stop reminding me. 5:08am... 5:09am... 5:10am. The door opens. There's the electric chair...

Safiya Rahman (12)
Stopsley High School, Luton

Time Bomber

I'm locked in a prison in space but I've nearly got all the items... I just need a clock and a cloak. The clock is easy. There's 1 outside but the cloak... I'll steal it from a guard. "Guard, guard, come here quick." I punch him hard, steal the cloak and make my time machine. "12, 11, 10, 9," I start chanting. I then disappear out of my cell and into time. To stop the police from finding me I blow up time turning into dust. The police find the dust and put that in prison just to make sure.

Harrison Iles (11)
Stopsley High School, Luton

CR7

It was the 2022 World Cup and it was the final. Portugal vs France. It's been 0-0 the whole game. Into extra time. Bernardo Silva breaks up play and dribbles past one defender and plays a beautiful ball into Ronaldo's path. 30 seconds left, he's taken it past 1 defender, 2 defenders then... foul. He was tripped over by the last defender. Free kick on the edge of the box. Last kick of the game. He's done it countless times before. All he has to do is put it in the back of the net. He steps up. He shoots...

Luke McCulloch (13)
Stopsley High School, Luton

Freeze Time At 17

I wish to freeze time at 17. Scared of ageing, I wish I could stay this way forever. When everything is easy, simple and fun. Growing means maturing, taking responsibility and learning from your mistakes. I'm currently 17. Once the clock strikes 12, it's all gonna be over. Just thinking about it sends shivers down my spine. What if I don't want to turn 18? Why don't I have a choice? This life full of fun and frolic is what I want - what I need! 5 minutes until 12 which is why I wish to freeze time at 17.

Amina Altaf (13)
Stopsley High School, Luton

The Explosion

I knocked. I knocked again. A strange sound from room 129 where my friend lives. I checked the message, room 129. Out of patience, I left it. Soon, I was to my last £1 and in the year 2172. The door I knocked on opened and never closed. It looked like a void inside. It was supposed to be Sunlight Hotel not dark. Then a loud siren said, "60 seconds left." I ran outside to check. There it was, a nuke so big that it could destroy the entirety of Earth. It was named '605'. It launched and exploded.

Kevin Fiaczyk (11)
Stopsley High School, Luton

Only 30 Seconds Left

Today is the 28th of October, 1985, and that is the date of Lexi's birthday. You see Lexi is a girl who goes to high school like everyone else and is 16 years of age. This day was supposed to be a nice day but it turned out not to be. It started with a sleepover, a bunch of friends having a good time until a conversation happened. Victor was his name, the mass killer of the so-called best school. The boy who took people into bathrooms and never returned. 30 seconds left till Lexi's birthday... 30 seconds left.

Mia Robertson (11)
Stopsley High School, Luton

The Hole

4289, this was the address. Heart pounding, sweat dripping, I walked towards the door, regretting my decision for working for the police department. I got closer. I pondered the question of what 4289 meant. Suddenly, before I knew it I was at the door. Heart pounding, sweat dripping, I turned the doorknob and with a deep breath, I forged through. As I looked around, I saw the truth. it was a trap. I looked down and saw an endless pit, engulfing everything I saw. Suddenly, I was pushed. I knew that this was the end...

Charlie Drein (11)
Stopsley High School, Luton

13 Monsters

13 monsters before me. Each one with vicious evil eyes. The cries and terror of the locals made me shiver and clench my jaw in defeat. How did I not see this coming? 13 natural disasters, 13 world wars, 13 new planets, 13 different ways to alert me and I still missed it. I clutched my gun in my right hand and turned around to face my team. Sweat dropped down from their foreheads, fear spread across their faces, all while being wide-eyed in anguish. "We can do this." We had to do this. We had no other choice.

Tara Akinwande (11)
Stopsley High School, Luton

2100

The year was 2099. I am going to try and save the world. Last year I tried but there was nothing I could do because no one would believe me. I went to my time travelling machine and typed 2100. "5, 4, 3, 2, 1, 0."
"Oh, I am in a news shop." I get a newspaper and read the news. It says, 'Breaking news, pandemic kills 300,000 people in 1 day'. "Oh no, I have to go back as soon as possible and tell everyone. I have to do this for me, for everyone. Mission... Save the World..."

Tahsin Sayed (13)
Stopsley High School, Luton

Seconds Left

35, 34, 33, 32, 31. Only 30 seconds left. Stop, let me catch you up. I was kidnapped and locked in a room. I woke up and I was caught. I didn't understand what to do till *tick-tock*. "Oh no, there is a timer." I had to escape now! I looked around. There was a door. I ran over. It was locked obviously so I looked around for a key. I found one but it didn't open. There was a box. "Yes!" It opened. *Tick-tock.* I ran to the door. 7, 6, 5. The key wouldn't turn. 3, 2, 1...

Skye Donovan (13)

Stopsley High School, Luton

Number 18

Stepping into the coffee shop, seeing a blank shadow in the distance, ordering her vanilla latte. After ordering she went to find a table to sit at. When she found a table her number was called out, number 18. As she went to collect her drink a man was heading to the till as well. Picking up the cup the man picked it up as well. Looking at each other their eyes met, realising it was love at first sight, smiling while they held eye contact. Suddenly they took each other's hands and went to sit down at a table.

Mary Kate Hughes (12)
Stopsley High School, Luton

Countdown

A dark room, one small red light blinked. No people. Silence! One day in the basement of an old, dilapidated house a bomb that nobody knew of lay on the plain concrete of the house's foundations. With a timer counting down it was only a matter of time before it went off. The months on the timer ticked away turning into weeks, the weeks turned to days, the days to hours, the clock flashed, the bold red numbers showed 2 hours left, quickly then flashing 1 hour, closely followed by 20 minutes, then detonation...

Aimee Moss (11)
Stopsley High School, Luton

One Penny

No! Why did I bet all my money? Is this it? I'm stupid. Urgh, time for my next loan from the bank. They must think I'm insane. Here I am, at my filthy house. Oh, what's that? A penny. Gee, thank god. Wait, it has a dead dog! They're one of a kind, I'm saved! Now I'm a millionaire. In an instant, I'm back here. Yes, hello, one round on the table. First bet, this penny's worth 1 million. The 2 dice roll out of my hands. The dice are resting on the table. I take a look. Snake eyes...

Ryan Holland (12)
Stopsley High School, Luton

1 Red Light

Down the corridor, she looks. 1 red light slowly flickers and Sofia walks to the red light. A cold breeze. A floorboard creaks on the way. Once she reaches it, the red light moves 1 more ahead. Sofia moves with it. It moves 1 more, ahead again. it happens again and again and again until she stops. A room door without a number on it. Sofia slowly opens the door. She is shocked. Knives on the dark cold wooden floors. Blood is smeared on the wall and letters are spread across the room spelling out 'run'...

Keila Ledaine (12)
Stopsley High School, Luton

Agent 372

I have been set up on a 'date' with Cameron Davler. He is oblivious and I, Millicent Thera, Agent 372, knows everything. It is half-past 6, he is late. Just as I planned. I rim his glass with toxins and poison, enough to kill a bear. After he arrives we talk for a while before our food arrives. I left for the bathroom, waiting for him to fall prey. I sit back down after a while and take a sip of my water... He swapped our glasses and I ingested the poison. "Enough to kill a bear. Agent 372..."

Amelia Cobaj (11)
Stopsley High School, Luton

The Phone Call

Midnight struck, the number called me again. I'd had enough. I gave up and answered. A muffled voice murmured, "Head to 77 Coven Garden immediately, I am watching you!" I got up and in a short space of time arrived, nobody answered. My patience got the better of me and I booted the door down. I laid my eyes upon a rusty key and safe. I didn't hesitate to open the safe and it led me to a location. I arrived and the war began. Shots were fired at me, I ran for my life, but I was being hunted...

Kian McGovern (11)
Stopsley High School, Luton

The 7 Crows

I stood alone, surrounded by trees. The sun was setting and I was lost in the forest. I had been followed by a man who I'd never seen before. It was getting dark. Really fast. I heard flapping above me. I looked up to see a line of birds. 7 crows. They watched me. They were directing me somewhere. *Snap!* I swirled round as I heard a twig break and my heart started racing. There was a shadow. The man. The crows started to cry and flew away. I followed the crows. I ran and ran as fast as possible.

Sumayya Mahmud (12)
Stopsley High School, Luton

Agent 58

There I was, Agent 58. Even had it written on my guns. I could feel the tension in the helicopter. If we didn't complete the mission it would all be over. The helicopter lowered down and we got out. The cold wind blew in our faces and then... the mission started. Our objective was to rescue the prisoners. All of my team ran in but no one was in sight. We were confused until *boom!* One of my teammates was shot in the back. We all ran to cover but he didn't make it. One man down. 5 versus 4...

Rayen Hart-Hernandez (13)
Stopsley High School, Luton

Intense Escape Room

I have woken up realising what just happened. I am 67 and the rest from 60 to 69 are here as well. We only had 10 minutes to escape. We couldn't find the solution to this note, which is our last one. 7 minutes left, and this started 23 minutes ago. This is terrifying! What should we do? We found a fingerprint, leading to the code. Yes! It worked! We managed to escape safely, everyone from 60 to 69. If you're wondering where we are, we're in an escape room. Goodbye for now, I will see you later.

Harrison Robins (13)
Stopsley High School, Luton

3:57am

It was 3:57am. I was in the car, the music blasting louder than the speed of light. I had so many missed calls but I didn't care. I pulled up to the nearest shop. I slammed the door shut, footsteps followed. At first, I didn't think anything of it. I went to the salad aisle and so did they. Are they following me? I ran out, got into my car. I pulled up on my drive thinking I had lost them. I went outside a few minutes later and guess what? There they were. It was 3:57am. Time hadn't changed...

Eliza Dobson (11)
Stopsley High School, Luton

The Last Day

Today is the last day on Earth. I'm number 53 out of 8 billion people. My time will end at 10:53pm. I will hopefully find a way to stop it from hitting Earth but there are no guarantees. I went to a shop to have a scrumptious last meal Suddenly, something caught my eye. It was a satellite station to show how far the asteroid is. I got a bomb and asked to plant the bomb into the rocket. The asteroid is 36 seconds away. Now 5, 4, 3, 2, 1, *boom!* The asteroid didn't explode. I am still alive.

Khateeja Malik (12)
Stopsley High School, Luton

How I Got Rick-Rolled By Number 25

One day, I was chilling playing Fortnite when all of a sudden I got a notification from a random number on my phone. They sent me a video, I didn't click the link because it could give me viruses. So I texted the number saying 'what is this and who are you?' they responded that they were called 25. I thought it was weird but went along with it anyway. They told me to click the link so I did.
Then I was disappointed to see what it was. It was Rick Astley 'Never Gonna Give You Up'!

Jack Weatherby (11)
Stopsley High School, Luton

7 Is Where?

CR7, the greatest of all time has gone missing. Is he dead? We all leave in tears, the press confused, the world confused. Floodlights blind us all from the evidence. We looked in all the houses. The first house, nothing, second house, nothing but next to the houses was a shack, in there was a phone on a chair, next to it was a lamp. *Ring, ring* was heard at 7am on the phone. I picked up the phone but nothing, it was silent. All we knew was that the thing that is calling is not human or is it...?

Ashtar Abbas Hussain (11)
Stopsley High School, Luton

Friday 13th

I'm number 13, the most hated number. To make it worse, today is Friday 13th. People believe that today should be an unlucky day. That's all I am, just a number. I don't even know who I am. But I just want people to know that there is nothing bad or unlucky about me. How is it possible? Why do people think these bad things about me? What did I do to make this happen? Every day is normal but not this day. I'm number 13, the most hated number. I don't even know what I am. Just a number.

Alessia Suciu (11)
Stopsley High School, Luton

For The 13th Time

I entered the elevator. Floor 13. The doors closed and I ascended. I walked to my room. 1313. I plugged my phone into the charger and went for a cold shower. Suddenly, it stopped and I heard a noise. When I got out, the first thing I did was grab my phone. It struck midnight. It was his birthday. I opened the fridge, got out a cake and added candles. I approached the closet with a smirk on my face and opened the doors. I placed the cake down and attempted to close the doors but he wouldn't let me...

Maahi Pattani
Stopsley High School, Luton

No Escape

I am number 97, I've been trapped in a small confined place. The TV suddenly turned on and it played a video. "Hello number 87, you have been tapped here for lying. You will now receive punishment if you cannot escape. Now, the question is, do you want to play a game?"
The TV turned off and something clamped on my leg. I only had a matter of minutes until a wire electrocuted me to death. I had to rip off my own leg... I screamed as my leg slowly ripped off but then it was too late...

Nahiyaan Ahmed (11)
Stopsley High School, Luton

The Lost Boy

It was 1962, there was a boy called Jammal. He woke up one day and his family was not there. He went outside and the sky was pitch-black and it was the morning. He looked around the town and there was nobody there. What had happened? Jammal went and knocked on his neighbour's door, no one replied. There was nobody at all. Jammal went back inside his house and tried to look for his cat but it was not there. Then Jammal realised something, he realised something he had never thought of, it's 1962.

Keyaan Chowdhoury (12)
Stopsley High School, Luton

Door Number 129

There is a knock, on door number 129. Jack opens it, he finds nobody there so he closes the door and looks behind. He sees someone in all black holding a knife. He screams so loud that people downstairs can hear him. There is a security guard near door number 135, he goes to 134 and the scream then gets closer and closer and closer until he stops at 129. The security guard sees blood coming out of the door, he starts to kick the door harder and harder and harder until it opens up and he sees Jack...

Gursehaz Hundal (12)
Stopsley High School, Luton

Prisoner

I've been imprisoned in this place my whole life. Ever since I have been number 64. I was a test subject. I always wanted to escape but the doors had a number passcode. Only workers knew it so today I was going to find out the passcode. After 64 minutes I saw a worker punch in 6469. I waited 4 to 6 minutes and escaped the living nightmare but what I saw next shocked me. A worker coming my way. I was freaking out so I hid behind a tree outside. Thankfully, the guard did not see and I'm gone.

Leila Jurevica (12)
Stopsley High School, Luton

The Kidnapping

There she was, it was a small abandoned house. Amber walked in holding her briefcase firmly. She was ready to give in to the kidnappers of her brother. She took a deep breath and reluctantly gave them the money but instead of them giving her brother Charlie back they knocked her out and locked her in room 269, put her on a chair and chained her hands and legs up.
When she woke up the room was cold and dark. "Where am I?" she said trying to break out of the chains that held her down.

Fopefunoluwa Onilude (11)
Stopsley High School, Luton

The End

It was the year 2153, I was driving home with my daughter, Lia when something happened... It has been 5 years since then. The end is creeping closer. My daughter was torn apart in front of my eyes. I'm scared, very scared. 5 minutes until the end. My family are dead. I don't know what to do. Will I survive? Will anyone survive? 2 minutes left. I've said my goodbyes to my friends. 10 seconds left. 9, 8, 7, 6, 5, 4, 3, 2... This is it, the end. 1... I closed my eyes and held my breath...

Melia Campbell (12)
Stopsley High School, Luton

24 Hours

24 hours to escape, 24 hours to plan. 24 hours until no more abuse, 24 hours to escape this abusive home of woman and man. 6 hours until 2am, 6 hours until freedom. 5 hours to find a phone, to call police to my home. 30 minutes until they arrive, 30 minutes to hide, 2 hours of explaining my story and until glory. 1 hour until my parents' arrest, 1 hour of searching my house and mess. 2 minutes until I'm freed, 1 minute until I take the lead. This cut like a knife, but I can now live life!

Hannah Ahmed (12)
Stopsley High School, Luton

The Mysterious Visit

9, 9 missed calls. I had no idea who had delivered these calls but it shook me to the core. *Knock, knock, knock.* I went to open the door but there was no one there. I closed the door and turned around. There it was. With my heart beating fast, my hand on my chest, I went to open the door so I could make a run for it. The creature growled looking very hungry and thirsty for blood. I rushed outside running for my life but before I knew it I'm on the floor being attacked by a monster...

Suriya Bahrololoumi (11)
Stopsley High School, Luton

Not-So-Lucky Number

7 is my lucky number. It's a heavenly number and 7 is the number of the gods. I don't understand. If 7 is my lucky number, why am I sitting here, holding on for dear life? Why can I feel my blood trickle down my back? I heard 7 footsteps. When I looked up, I realised that those were the footsteps of my enemy. They crouched down to stare me in the eyes. They put their cold hand on my face and before I knew it, the last sentence I heard was: "You're not so lucky now, are you?"

Ivlia Maria Costinivc (14)
Stopsley High School, Luton

Multiversal Mystery

Earth 616, the 6th of September 4200. Night-time. Nobody was around. Strange. I saw a countdown. 3, 2, 1. Then it happened. Someone had fallen onto the ground. It woke up. It had a knife! I ran! I saw an open door. Door 69. I locked myself in. I was safe or was I? The house was tiny. I knew that it would be here soon. I found a note. It said, 'Earth 616, my life's work. This experiment has gone horribly wrong. In the year 4200, we all die unless...' Then I heard a bang. I blacked out.

Yusuf Careem (11)
Stopsley High School, Luton

Living Nightmare

7. An odd number. Eyes staring at me. Whispers are all I hear. I look at my wrist. The number 7 is engraved. The damned 7. Who knew that a number could determine your fate? Out of all the people, I got the odd number. I was unfortunate. Suddenly, the police entered. Jumping off stage, I ran. I ran out of the hall, running from this nightmare. I stopped at a hill. There was no escape. Police behind me. Closing my eyes I counted to 3. I woke up, drenched in sweat. I looked at my wrist. 7 is there.

Adeena Chowdhury (12)
Stopsley High School, Luton

The Hallway

I looked left and right. Up and down. I was scared. My heart dropped. The lights were flickering. It was just me in a dark, scary, gloomy hallway. It was silent. If a pin dropped I would hear. Down the hallway, I heard a voice. It told me to come closer. I gulped. I was so frightened that my sweat was coming off me and my throat was hurting. I walked closer and closer to the voice as my legs were shaking. I wanted to turn around and run away but then 50 men were suddenly there looking at me...

Jonathan McLean (13)
Stopsley High School, Luton

The Battle!

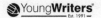

I woke up. "Where am I? I don't know. I am trapped." I saw a door, I opened it. I ducked. A bullet shot over my head. I saw the gunner. I told him to shoot the gun. *Bang!* It hit another tank. They shot, and it missed. After that, we shot and before we did we drove over a rock. We missed. Just then they shot. Then *boom!* We got hit and destroyed. We failed, I failed. I managed to get out of the tank. I saw we had 100 or more tanks left but they had 300 tanks...

Joshua Hough (12)
Stopsley High School, Luton

Cursed Floor

Floor 9... where hundreds met their doom. The rumours say that this floor has been defined as the cursed one. I walked out of the elevator stepping onto the creaky wooden floor. I always clean this floor in a rush hoping my days would not come to an end. As always I grabbed my cloth and spray and started cleaning the dusty desks in a rush. As I cleaned the lights flicked for a second. Being me I brushed it off as nothing. But I should have listened to them. "Help me, please..."

Aleeza Khan (11)
Stopsley High School, Luton

Life Is A Game

They say cats have 9 lives, chess has 32 chess pieces, 16 per side. My mum used to tell me life is a game of chess. If you make the wrong move you'll die, if you make the right one, you'll survive. Never let your opponent get too close to your queen, your heart. Let me give you some advice, never fall in love. Love is a game. If you lose, you may never be able to fall in love again. 9 lives, cats can withstand falls that would easily kill a human. I am confused. So what about me?

Rojai Wedderburn-Smith (13)
Stopsley High School, Luton

The 19 Minute Race

It was 1919, and the massive race was there number 19. My head dropped to my feet as I was trying to get the best start. The light was as red as blood. It turned yellow. I focused. It wasn't turning green. It fell on me. It turned green. I pressed the accelerator, climbing 19, 90, 1900. I kept getting faster. 19 was in the lead. I floored it. I started to hear my 1919 turbos kick in. I was almost done. *Boom!* I won. I will never forget the 19 minute race. Number 19 is a pro.

Jonathan Asaam Baroka (12)
Stopsley High School, Luton

Poker

It was 11 o'clock and I was on my 3rd drink of the night. I had rolled a 6. I felt confident... I went all in. I was against a blonde lady wearing red. She showed no emotion on her face; she was impossible to read. I felt dizzy and my eyes kept unfocusing, the lights were blurring into lines. I saw the lady's face shift to a smile as she looked me in the eyes and smirked. She had the best hand I'd ever seen... I had lost. Drunk out of my mind, I left, handing her my money.

Georgina Harriman (14)
Stopsley High School, Luton

The End?

1 minute, 1 minute until the police arrive. Why did I get myself into this? How did I get myself into this? I'm only 13. I don't want to die. 30. 30 seconds left, is this the start of my life or the end...? Am I gonna make it? Am I not? There are only 7 of us. There's an army out there. The robbers start praying, but this isn't the time to pray. 0. Zero seconds left. Mum, I promise if I get out of this bank I am going to stop. I'm going to change my life forever.

Raoul Mavris (11)
Stopsley High School, Luton

The Test

We have 1 hour and 15 minutes until the end of the test, and I was still on number 2. I was struggling so hard, but the only thing on my mind was lunch, other than that my brain was empty. I tried to be slick and look at my partner's work, but he was already halfway done. Every second, every minute, I looked at the clock, hoping that it was lunch. Then I thought to myself, *what if I actually focus?* Within the blink of an eye I was 91. Then it was lunch. I had finished.

Zaynab Safa (11)
Stopsley High School, Luton

Room 237

I stared down at my name tag. That's all I saw. Sweat was dripping down my forehead. A spine-tickling shiver travelled on my peculiar spine. Everyone said I was public enemy number one or so I thought. Only 30 seconds left until I was called. "Number 17 you're up," stated the officer. With every step I took, I felt like all eyes were on me. I felt engulfed in a series of mixed emotions. After what felt like an eternity I was there. Room 237. What happens next...?

Josiah Olayinka (11)
Stopsley High School, Luton

Sweet 16... Or Is It?

It was the 16th of August, the day of my 16th birthday when I got the message. '16 lies. 16 tries. 16 dies'. I thought it was just some little joke or prank so I just forgot about it. *Click!* Gone. Out. Bye... But now I know it definitely wasn't a joke or a prank. It was real. I don't know how or why or who but I know it is true. I did lie, a horrible lie. I did try to cover it up. I did die, a horrendous death... I guess sweet 16s aren't sweet at all.

Aisha Khan (11)
Stopsley High School, Luton

Room 309

3/09. My first day of university. I don't like this place. It's so different here. To make matters worse, I can't find my class. I cannot be late on my first day, what would my professor think? As I turn the corner to make my way down a long corridor, I'm met with some piercing eyes. As he asks for my name, I get lost in his aura. As we walk to class we begin to open up to each other. We reach room 309 and I take my seat. I think I'm going to like it in here.

Ellie Brown (13)
Stopsley High School, Luton

World Cup

I was number 7, sprinting as fast as I could towards the goal. Was I going to score? I passed to number 8 who then passed to me when I was in the box. This was it. Without thinking, I kicked the ball as hard as I could into the goal. I thought the keeper was going to save it. I lost all my hope. It was 3-3 with 5 seconds left. The goalie dived as the ball went in. My team automatically started cheering. I had scored the winning goal of the match. We shook hands and cheered more.

Bri'yani Grant (11)
Stopsley High School, Luton

The Disappearance

It was Friday the 13th and Mary was asleep on her couch. While Mary was asleep 3 men came and kidnapped her and took her to a mysterious building. When she woke up she found herself wearing a tracksuit with the number 1313 on it, thinking it was her name. As she explored she found a few friends named 2098 and 2099 (Mia and Riley). They had a plan to escape with a crowbar and as soon as she escaped she woke up on her couch with the crowbar in her hand. Was she really in a dream?

Karina Sypytkowska (11)
Stopsley High School, Luton

The Day I Turned 17

As soon as I turned 17 I rented an apartment on the 17th floor, number 17. I had school the next day, so I decided to go to sleep early since it was already late. Before I knew it, I was fast asleep.
I was awoken by a strange noise. So I opened my eyes, just to close them the next second. I saw a deformed creature, it whispered, "17," in my ear. Then I screamed as my ear was bitten.
17. 17. 17.
Then I opened my eyes to see I was in a hospital bed...

Emilia Stochla (12)
Stopsley High School, Luton

The Gamble Of Fate

All eyes were on me. I sat on the chair in the middle of the casino. I placed all my money on one pathetic bet. My sweaty hands were holding the dice, this number would decide my fate. I rolled the dice, it slowly tumbled over. My eyes were blurry and I had hard, heavy breathing. I could feel the tension in the air. I saw 3 pairs of black dots on the dice. The number was 6. Sweat trickled down my face. The only thing on my mind was the number 6. My life is saved. I had won.

Mehnaz Kudhbudeen (11)
Stopsley High School, Luton

The Deserted Hotel

It all happened in room number 36. A couple of weeks ago I planned to travel to England. I booked a room in a hotel but found no receptionist. I found keys on the desk for room number 36. I entered the room but found nothing inside. I heard the door open and then suddenly felt a rush of wind behind me. It happened so quickly that I don't know who or what did it. My last vision was seeing my blood rush out of my body slowly spreading all across the ground in front of me.

Sarah Samara (12)
Stopsley High School, Luton

Unknown

I am number 22, in an empty hotel. I did not think anything of how empty it was but then I went up to my room which was 306. I knocked but there was no answer. I was checking if there was some sort of note. I kept looking and saw a message saying 'If you want you and your family to live come to room 22'. My heart immediately started pounding with fear. I had so many questions to ask myself but before I did I charged into room 22 feeling terrified. It was empty...

Josie Hill (12)
Stopsley High School, Luton

The 13th Shooter

There was a shooter that was among 13 students. The only clue left behind was a thick piece of brown hair. The kids with brown hair were Alex, Maria, Liam, Junior, Kim, Ibrahim, Henry, Grace, Brandon, Emily, Connor, Daria and Farhim. They all were the only suspects in the class. In order to see who it was they had to do 3 quizzes. They were about their breakfast, clothes and night routine. They all passed apart from one person. Can you guys guess who the shooter is...?

Huja Bawor (12)
Stopsley High School, Luton

The £5 Heist

I was down to my last £5. The bill was £6 and there was no way I could convince the worker to accept £5. I didn't know what to do. In panic, I shoved £5 in the worker's hand and sprinted through the doors. I couldn't stop running and from the corner of my eye, I spotted security behind me. I ran into an alley and hid behind a dumpster. While I was in there I felt some change in my pocket. It was a £1 coin. All that for nothing.

Mariam Ahmad (11)

Stopsley High School, Luton

Day 368

I am number 4. It is day 368 of being by myself on this spacecraft. Nobody else has woken up from their capsules. I have to stay in the largest room on the spacecraft (222). I am provided with good water and electronics. I spend hours in there trying to figure out how I can survive until I reach Planet Ezlon. I only go out of my room for breakfast, lunch and dinner. But something has been happening with my oxygen, it has been running low. What will happen next...?

Keyra Nardani (12)
Stopsley High School, Luton

Upside Down

2099, that was it! If only I knew then she would have still been here. I've got this new case, I can't say much but I need to find a code. The thing is I have these dreams of numbers, the code, but when I wake up I forget. 2099. How did I know that? I see the number everywhere, it's my door number. How didn't it cross my mind? As I sat alone on my bed holding 2099. I turned it over, 6602. Now I remember this was the code! 6602, yes, she is saved!

Safa Khalid (12)
Stopsley High School, Luton

30 Seconds Till Home Time

Only 30 seconds left until home time. I can't wait. I can play on my Xbox all evening.
Just 30 seconds.
I can imagine it.
29, 28, 27... it is so close.
30 seconds has gone, it is time. I pick up my bag and put on my coat. Everyone darts out of the door. It is like an all-out war. People are getting knocked around like baseball bats, some people are even falling on the floor. I can see the gate. I am close. Will I make it? Will I make it?

Ethan Ledster (11)
Stopsley High School, Luton

The Delay

It's December 3rd. I'm in shock. You see, a week ago I was preparing to go to London for the holidays. But last minute, there was a delay; we missed the coach and were late to the flight. I was shattered; now we had to wait 3 more weeks to go again! But now, watching the news, I'm realising it might've saved my life. Apparently, there was a plane crash at Heathrow Airport just after I couldn't go. I feel... extremely lucky. Thank goodness!

Katey Ocansey Kwapong-Kumi (12)
Stopsley High School, Luton

My Demise, Number 13

I wake up, eyes blurred, all I can think is, *13*. My eyes unblurred. All I could see was a corridor, what happened to me? Nothing filled my head. I looked at my wrists, 13:13. Why this? I accepted my fate. One thought came to my mind, *go to room 13*. I had nothing to lose so I decided to go to room 13.
10, 11, 12... sweat dripped down my face.
I opened the door and blacked out. It was an endless loop. How was I going to break this?

Adam Malik (11)
Stopsley High School, Luton

Prison Break

My name is inmate 5755. I used to have a normal life, until it happened. I was down to my last fiver. I was in desperate need of some money so I joined a gang, that was the worst decision of my life because I got caught. I got told to rot away in prison.
I'd had enough of prison so I decided to escape. I had my whole plan set out, little did I know someone would steal it. Now the only thing left is my inmate number. It was my own brother.

Mamusu Conteh (11)
Stopsley High School, Luton

100 Minutes

100 minutes to kill 100 people. 3, 2, 1, it had begun. Fighters came charging with their spears, swords, guns and axes. People dying was heard. I caught a glance of a bloodbath while running to escape. One down, killed by a gun; another down, 98 left; 97, 96, 95. People were falling dead like dominoes, one by one. 94, 93, 92, 91, 90. Weapon. I needed a weapon to defend myself. I thought, *will I be next? Will I be the last one standing?*

Amanda Kalu (11)
Stopsley High School, Luton

Room 200 Was Empty

I work as a cleaner in a retirement home. I normally clean 10 rooms every shift. I came along room 200 and a putrid smell was slivering its way out. Of course, I had to check it, but no one was there. There was nothing. Suddenly, I heard a screech coming from the bathroom. I thought it was Mary stuck on the toilet again. But it wasn't. My soul left my body the immediate second it glared at me. I didn't know if I should scream or cry...

Kiyla West (12)
Stopsley High School, Luton

Escape Room

There were only 60 seconds left.
The eerie clown was staring at me with a grin full of bloodlust. Various shivers ran through my spine as there were only 30 seconds left until doom. *Tick-tock, tick-tock.* The time was disappearing quicker than a heartbeat.
15 seconds left.
The clown whipped out a kitchen knife and started juggling it around. I started saying my last prayers as the clock was getting closer to 0...

Melody Igbinovia (11)
Stopsley High School, Luton

Spooky 303

It was the scariest day in the world. Me and my friends chose a hotel that looked nice, as we thought. Our room looked pretty. It was number 303. We had heard myths that said anyone who came to this hotel went missing, but we didn't believe it.
In the night, I heard a scream in another room. I went to see what the noise was and found the dead bodies of my friends. I called the police but they didn't know who it was.

Kseniia Kamnieva (11)
Stopsley High School, Luton

Board Game Chase

I opened my eyes. A board game. I looked around, someone was behind me. A dice appeared in my hands. I had to roll. I rolled a 5, 5 forward. Maybe a 2, 6, 4, 1, 3, the chances were random. It was still behind me. I felt my heartbeat racing. It was just a game. Though it didn't seem friendly. I could see the end. I was 6 tiles away. I rolled a 4. It rolled a 3. I needed to roll a 2. I rolled a 1. Game Over. Was this death?

Laura Markiewicz (12)
Stopsley High School, Luton

5 Minutes

Only 5 minutes left. I rushed through the door to find something unexpected. There in front of my eyes was a creepy doll with blood all over her face, dancing like she had never danced before. She walked closer to me. Time was running out fast. I had 3 minutes left to take out the doll's batteries. I ran as fast as a cheetah towards the doll.
Boom! She exploded...
That wasn't meant to happen.

Eshal Hussain (11)
Stopsley High School, Luton

The Game

Only 30 seconds left on the clock, the time was ticking. We all rushed towards it. The thing we were fighting for since the very beginning. Chris fell over the platform and died instantly from the blades. With my adrenaline pumping, I rushed to it and shoved everyone away. I finally grabbed it and I saw a blinding light shine over me. It was the most beautiful thing I'd ever laid my eyes upon. It was my freedom.

Ibrahim Uddin (11)
Stopsley High School, Luton

World Cup

It was the 90th minute and I am 99 years old and I have to win this match. It was the World Cup and I have to win this penalty. Okay, here I go... and I suddenly score! This is it. I have won it! I have won it! Now I can relax from this tiring match. So yes, I have done it, and now it is time for the gold trophy. Here we go. It is time. I hug everyone and shake hands with the other team and say goodbye to football.

Mdnafiz Alam (12)
Stopsley High School, Luton

Integer

Pokédex number 152. Chikorite, aka me.
I woke up, looked at my arms and immediately knew something was wrong. They were all short and stubby. I got out of bed and was walking on 4 legs. I looked in the mirror and I was Chikorita. I went downstairs and found a mysterious potion. I picked it up and drank it. I was enveloped in a white glow. I looked in the mirror and found I was back to normal.

Taylor Price (11)
Stopsley High School, Luton

The Room

It's been 237 days, I think. I finally escaped room 12, but something else is in here, something different. It's after me, I can feel it coming closer. I have to go soon. It's here, I can see it, it looks like a shadow, its body dark but translucent, its head is a scribble just like one a child makes. Oh no... it's seen me. I must go now...

Liv Stones (12)
Stopsley High School, Luton

The Worst 11th Birthday

It was a cold windy and rainy morning on Saturday. Fria's mum woke up to prepare food for her 11th birthday. It was 3 in the afternoon so her dad and she went to buy a cake. They went back home after they got the cake. As soon as they got home, Fria's dad started arguing about the cake with her mum. Fria ran upstairs to her room and started crying.

Mir Sabiha Islam (12)
Stopsley High School, Luton

The Hidden Door

I turned left, then right. Nothing... Still blocked in their stupid maze. I tried to walk faster but I felt dizzy. Suddenly, I saw the number 10. Maybe it was a clue... It moved... It was a secret door... I entered the hidden room. Once inside I couldn't believe what I saw... there was nothing... The room was empty... How am I going to escape?

Alexia Creciunescu (13)
Stopsley High School, Luton

Error 404

It finally happened; I thought it never would. It exists. The artificial superintelligence; and it's wrecking, no, terminating our civilisation.
NeoTech had already been dubious, suddenly bouncing up like a coiled spring with all their masses of 'innovative' technology - but what they made worked, so nobody questioned them. Enormous mistake. Turns out they'd been collecting data from all of us - enough to finally create the end of days.
I don't know how many are left. Millions? Thousands? It doesn't matter now; just survive...
I check my phone: 'ERROR 404: HUMANS NOT FOUND'. Are they... all gone? Am I even... human?

Robbie Eckley (13)
Taunton School, Taunton

3 Seconds

I stood there, only rags left of my clothes. Around me were shards of smashed glass and bricks that had fallen from tall, ancient buildings. Corpses were lying on the ground, not budging in the concrete wrecks of once-beautiful constructions. With numb fingers from countless, dreadful fights, I clambered up the scaffolding of one of the last upright skyscrapers, the sign saying 'Moonview Resort', hanging limply from one rope. Once I eagerly hauled myself up to the third floor, I found what I was searching for. A bag of explosives, with a timer saying 00:03. I was too late.

Brodir Schmör (13)
Taunton School, Taunton

I Am Number 24

I survived. I have cuts all over my body. I can see the white walls of the hospital. The doctor walks over to me. She says something to me, but I can't understand her. "What happened?" I asked.
"You survived," she replied.
"You're the 25th person to survive."
Suddenly, there was a noise next to me. *Beep, beep, beep.* All the doctors in the room rushed over to the beep. After a few minutes of silence and waiting, the doctor came back over to me. The only thing she said was, "You are the 24th person to survive."

Maddie Hudgell (13)
Taunton School, Taunton

24-48 Hours...

"This is Andy Jackson, BBC News... Nuclear bombs are in position. Sources tell us that, if Putin chooses, many parts of the world could be decimated within the next 24-48 hours." His voice is a cracked series of broken syllables, his face crumples as he stops speaking. He is not looking at the camera now. His hands start to shake. He discards his cue cards on the desk in front of him. This cannot be happening. It's the stuff of nightmares and dystopian novels, not 21st century reality. The screen goes black. Distant bombs thud. It is really happening...

Mollie Fox (13)
Taunton School, Taunton

Room 237 Was Empty

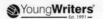

Standing there in the dark, desolate street, dim lights flickering behind me, I glared up at the colossal structure looming over me. I strode forward, carelessly splashing through the murky puddles forming from the endless heavy downpour of rain. Reaching for the handle, I noticed the door left ajar. Cautiously, I drew a Glock from the inside of my jacket and stepped forward, kicking the door open as I went. Gun locked and aimed at the ready, I rapidly ascended the steep steps of the eerie stairwell. I turned the corner and burst into the room. Room 237 was empty.

Wilbur Grundy (13)

Taunton School, Taunton

20.4.99, 16:43

I awoke, in a tank of transparent liquid. I wore a gas-like mask, I could feel it running down my throat gagging me. Shadowed figures approached the glass door. They wore white jumpsuits covering every inch of their faces and figures as an echo bellowed through my ears. I frantically called to be freed, a suited woman came rushing through a herd of white. She took a moment to admire as I watched her breath slowly condensate the glass. She let out a few words in shock. "She's awake, first in 100 years. 20.4.99, 16:43. Someone, write it down."

Blythe Browning (14)

Taunton School, Taunton

Room 237 Was Empty

How could it happen? It couldn't be real? No. The most dangerous criminal nowadays had disappeared from the room in my charge. How? A million questions surrounded my brain. There weren't any windows, materials, pills, or anything. The entire night, I was in front of the door, the only way to escape. I didn't hear anything at all, sounds, noises, squeaks. What will happen to my job? It was my most important position so far. I need to find this astute man and the manner he broke out. This room has a mystery. My obligation is to find it, 237.

Paola De Pedro (13)
Taunton School, Taunton

24.02.2022

It's 5am. *Boom!* You run to the corridor; your parents are already there. In your mind, you see everything now for real. Everything you've learned and feared about war is now on your doorstep. Your body is shaking. Nobody knows what to do. You are confined to the basement of your house, while your father patrols your city. You don't know if your country will survive. If you will see your father again. Whether there will be a tomorrow. If only this was just a nightmare, but it's real, it's here and it's not going away.

Nazarii Pavlyk (13)
Taunton School, Taunton

Only 30 Seconds Left...

Only 30 seconds left, that's all I had. 30 seconds left before everything was over, 30 seconds left before I was caught. Let me explain how I got into this situation. I woke this morning to a blatant thumping at my door. "Open up kid, we know you're in there!" Panic overwhelmed me and I jolted out of bed. I knew that I needed to escape, get away from these people. I looked towards my window, instincts kicking in and jumped, then ran, faster than ever before. But they were catching up, only 30 seconds left before I'd be caught.

Daisy Challacombe (14)
Taunton School, Taunton

10 Seconds

There are only 30 seconds left. My hands gripping the lock; trying any possible number that could open to the outside world. My lungs yearning for oxygen, the lightheaded feeling is finally hitting me. The toxic air seeping through my mask. It is nearly game over. My heart dropping into my stomach, I could feel the beating of it racing. The echo of the odious beasts rises from the base of the stairs. The unbroken ticking of the clock, my whole body is shaking. Was this going to be the day that I died? Thoughts clustering my mind. 10 seconds!

Chloe De Jager (13)
Taunton School, Taunton

4 Digits

I met you at a train station, had nowhere to go, you never asked about me, but that night when I woke up you left leaving me with nothing, disappeared out of my life. I'm losing my mind, blaming myself, waiting for you to come back. Your words are stuck in my head, repeatedly talking to me, and every sentence eventually sounds like a number. What is it? Maybe co-ordinates or phone number. But as time passes and the memories within it, disappearing leaving an empty space. You drove me crazy but why am I suffering from struggles so much?

Lana Kalyuzhna (13)
Taunton School, Taunton

You Can't Win

13. I am... number 13. That's all they think of me. A digit. An integer. Nothing more, nothing less. Every day we have our souls drained out of us. They torture us, they torment us. And for what? Science. We are experiments. Guinea pigs. Used for our power. This isn't a life! Can't they see we are so much more than tests? Than toys? The girls before me have failed. And I'm next. Their last chance. 13. The lucky number. If I fail, they fail. I know I can do it. Revolutionise science. But I can't let them destroy me.

Kaitlin Chacko (13)
Taunton School, Taunton

13

"13!" Eyes wide open. Echoes. It's cold and I can feel the tiles against my bare skin. I can't see anything besides an open window at the top of the room framing a full moon in the dark sky. Resounding screams catch up to me. I recognise it, remember it. A crow screeches in my ear making my eardrums wince. Lying on the bathroom floor desperate for someone to find me, I can hear the distant howling wolves and the piercing shriek of an owl. My memory is blank. The only thing occupying the empty space is a number... 13.

Charlotte Webber (13)
Taunton School, Taunton

Room 99

I screamed, "Stop, please stop, don't do this!" I woke up to a light bulb held by a thread and a room in front of me that had 99 scraped viciously on the door. I heard a sweet angelic voice saying, "Lexi, Lexi." It sounded so familiar but so new all at once. I approached the door, it creaked with great sound and saw my mother. I went to collapse into her arms but there was nothing. I screamed, "Mum, Mum! Please come back! Don't do this again to me! I will be better, don't send me back again!"

Arthur Wilkinson (13)
Taunton School, Taunton

30 Seconds

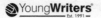

30 seconds left... Sweat rushed down my blood-covered body like a rampant buffalo. The tick of the clock rang around my head, as the dread of realisation ran throughout my mind. I was going to die. My legs buckled at the thought, I felt the sting of tears as they trickled down my shaking face. 15 seconds... Blood swam around my veins as panic filled up rapidly within me. My limp body fell against the lifeless wall, my vision blurred with tears. 5.... Here it is, 4... 3... My final moments lay ahead, 2... I'm so sorry, I... Clara.

Charlie Webber (15)

Taunton School, Taunton

I Rolled A 6

I rolled a 6 in a game like Jumanji. The dice were alien. 29 sides. The pawn moved forward, closer to the end, closer to danger, closer to death. It stopped. The strange holographic image of a being unknown to all but me. It began to speak in that raspy, scratchy, almost indistinguishable voice. "A 6, a good number for your people, a bad number for you. Your time is near, whether good or bad, the bridge is almost made." The walls collapsed, the roof, however, remained in the sky. I rolled again. it was 13. I felt the roof.

Sebastian Parvin (14)
Taunton School, Taunton

First To 10Gs

I was so close. I had hoped for this day for years. I've been getting higher and higher Gs over the past year, each week. After the maintenance, I had gone faster and eventually, I reached 9G, recently I made it up to 9.9G. When I say I made it, really the engineers did it. I'll be the first to reach 10Gs and it will happen today, a special day, 4th June 2026. Today I will reach it. The first human ever, of course, 10G has been reached before unmanned, but I'm the first human ever, in Earth's extensive history.

Thomas Dutton (14)
Taunton School, Taunton

Sector 23

I looked out, gazing across the rows of identical cells, each containing a man more or less like me. Each with a story to tell. I grabbed a bar in my right hand, slumping against the grimy grey brickwork of my cell and sighed. I had been stuck behind the same identical bars for 4 years. I found myself wondering how the world would have changed while I'd been gone. I had changed. For better or for worse, that's what prisons do. Well, ready or not here I come 'cause tonight is the night I break out of Sector 23.

Zachary Roberts (13)
Taunton School, Taunton

The Escape

There was none. No escape from my fate. I needed to leave but couldn't. I was trapped. They're hot on my heels. I looked up and noticed there was a hole in the ceiling. It was ten metres up but I think I can make it. With the last of my strength, I leapt up and landed on the roof. My escape was near. I sprinted away from the complex into the woods. Who knew what danger lay ahead but it was better than getting caught. Their car lights were blinding but I continued running. There's no place that's safe.

Kristofer Maskell (13)
Taunton School, Taunton

I Rolled A 6

I didn't mean to kill her. The headmaster is standing next to me while everyone's surrounding the lifeless body. The room is filled with silence. My breath is now heavier, as I hold a single card. I could feel it from the beginning. I should've stepped out of this right when I felt the ice-cold air grasp my neck, once the Ace of Spades appeared in my hand. My palms had to close however, all I was able to do was hear an insistent tone echoing from inside my head. A number that caused so much. I rolled 6.

Hrista Chakova (13)
Taunton School, Taunton

I Am 2099

I awake from my sleep, unsure where I am. My vision blurs, my shoulder cramps. I observe my unfamiliar surroundings as I stumble out of bed. I peer out of a nearby window to see no one. Not one person, not even a car. Looking closer, I catch a glimpse of my reflection. My hair is no longer past my shoulders, a scar chokes my neck and on my shoulder is... 2099. 2099. The numbers are indelible in my mind and now on my skin. It was the year that everything changed. The year that people suffered... because of me.

Chloe Kavanagh (14)
Taunton School, Taunton

I Was Always Second, Until Today

All my life, I was never the best. Born gifted with the genetics that made my dad such an elite athlete, but so was my brother. As close as I came to number 1, he always beat me in every aspect of life. This evening was my chance. After 19 years of pure grind and competition, our final challenge, the 2024 NBA draft. It was now our turn to continue our father's legacy. The announcer had our destiny in hand. "With the first pick the Lakers choose..." You can guess the rest, I was now number 1.

Adel Elidrissi (14)
Taunton School, Taunton

My Number 2

My story is inspired by the number 2. With 2 feet, life is full of choices. Choices were made easy because I was free. With 2 feet I could stand for hours in a queue at a theme park to get on a thrilling ride. I could shop for hours. I could compete with my teammates and friends. I could get from one classroom to another whilst laughing and sending a chat. But now I only have 1 that works my choices are harder, painful and tiring, dependent on others. 2 is stronger than 1, don't wish to be alone.

Harper Oliver Whittaker (13)
Taunton School, Taunton

Apartment 385

I woke up next to my beautiful wife and children lying by my side, watching TV. Suddenly, I felt as though I was being dragged through a portal. The faded image of my family in the back of my mind. Then I awoke laid in a lab. I struggled free of the strange goggles on my eyes and ran out of the building. I darted through the streets of London, until I reached the apartment block. I raced up the stairs and burst through the door and it hit me. None of it was real, as apartment 385 was empty!

Alexa Wiltshire (13)
Taunton School, Taunton

Room 237 Was Nothing

Suddenly, I am running on the pavement. I trip; falling into an endless series of rooms each numbered 237. I look around. I am horrified by what is behind me. The tinted glow of a smiling face hovers towards me. Its dark body twists and turns in the claustrophobic corridor. I shuffle my body through this compact, endless space. Still, the creature twists and swirls its boneless body behind me. It is closing in on me now; I have to make a choice. I turn the handle of the nearest door...

Samuel Webber (13)

Taunton School, Taunton

How Much Longer?

13 seconds. 13 minutes. 13 hours. 13 years. How much longer? The constant beat of my heart reverberated around the room. As I lay, I felt the damp dirtiness start to soak into my already hideous clothes. But why should I care? No one will ever see me again. I have had no human contact in over 13 years, well it depends if you count footsteps and food deliveries. They keep me alive, but they leave me to go insane. Am I a science experiment? I glanced at my wrist; I am number 13, why me?

Amarra Beviss (14)
Taunton School, Taunton

I Was Down To My Last £5

I was down to my last £5. I had nearly finished stuffing my duffel bag full of cash, everyone was on the ground, some screaming and some crying. My whole life I had lived on the streets with nobody caring what could happen to me, but then I saw the sirens and they started to appear outside. The flashing of the blue and the red was making me feel dizzy and lightheaded and my vision began going all blurry until I felt my body give up on me. That is when my life changed forever.

Jasmine Bolland (13)
Taunton School, Taunton

1 Minute Left

The relentless timer ticks down. My sweaty palms try to stop it the best I can. Only 60 seconds left. What do I do? How do I stop it? How? How? My mind searches for a solution, the years of training didn't lead me to this. "Not like this," I shout, as the timer hit 30... I cut the green wire hoping, praying it will work, but the timer speeds up. '19, 18, 17', race across the screen. "It's a double circuit!" I say...

Carlton Chu (14)
Taunton School, Taunton

30 Seconds Left

I have a dream. My whole life I have been waiting for this, it's right here in front of me, a huge bank ready to be opened. The code? I turned the lock a few times and that was it, 3030. I have it, all that money. Inside was a letter, a letter informing me that I have 30 seconds to live. 30 seconds to do what? I thought for a bit. I could build a time machine to go and see my favourite person, I had to go back to 1990 and there he was.

Jack Blackwell (13)
Taunton School, Taunton

13

She fumbled with the keys to house 13 whilst chatting with her friend over the phone. "It's such a coincidence, house 13 and it's the 13th!" she said cheerily.

"Yeah, but it's Friday," her friend murmured.

"Ha! How ironic! Anyway, wanna grab some lunch tomorrow?" she asked.

As the door creaked open, she saw the abandoned house again. She placed boxes upon boxes in the kitchen, soon feeling hungry.

Creeakk!

"What was that?" she panicked.

That night, she woke with a jolt, hearing something. "Oh, just the dog," she mumbled.

But little did she know, it wasn't the dog...

Melda Yilmaz (11)

Unity College, Towneley Holmes

Need For Speed!

Lane 7 has always been lucky for me. Deep breath. There was silence in the stadium. 90,000 people crammed into the Paris arena. My fingers started to ache under the pressure of my weight.
"On your marks, get set, go!"
I exploded out of the blocks, the wind flattened my hair. The crowd roared, Speed, I am Speed. This was my last chance to win gold. I pushed, using all my strength and willpower. I could see the finish line, I dived head-first through the finish line. I looked at the clock... new world record, beating Usain Bolt. Gold!

Ben Mayhew (13)
Unity College, Towneley Holmes

13-21-18-4-5-18

The doorbell rang. Once. Twice. Impatiently, they entered. Not knowing who it was, I peered around the wall. It was clear that he was after me, but what for? my terror-stricken mind wondered. I heard his boots thud as he ascended the staircase. I knew he was getting closer and closer to me. Then it came to me. Of course, how had I not thought of it before? Immediately, I tiptoed along the corridor to the safe behind my grandfather's portrait and entered the code. 13-21-18-4-5-18. I knew I only had one choice and that was to m-u-r-d-e-r him.

Ben Marsden (15)
Unity College, Towneley Holmes

143 - I Love You

The note she held could change everything and she'd sink in the blink of an eye. Finally, gaining a bit of courage she gently opened it. 'Night-times were bright, daytimes were dark, nothing but this passionate love could ever make a spark. Nothing made sense in this world, nothing ever would, but when I was with you everything would. Now, my dear, I have to go. There's just one thing you must know, 143 I love you so. Forever with me repeat the words 143'. Hope filled her. "He's not dead, I know it."

Hollie Barton (14)
Unity College, Towneley Holmes

The Exit

13. That's all I am now, isn't it? Ever since that day back at the lab. Maybe I should explain a bit. But first, we travel back to 2099, where it all began. I awoke in a strange, dimly-lit room. I tried to stand but thick, bronze cuffs held my wrists and ankles still. I looked down to find myself sat in a medical chair. A faint source of light glowed from somewhere in the room. A cruel, cackling laughter echoed all around me. My heart sank as the glow faded away. The only way out, my only exit...

Freya Iddon (11)
Unity College, Towneley Holmes

Number 1 Horror

Once upon a time, the end. No, it's not the end, that was the first sentence, the first word. Nothing ends that quickly. This is a story about a number 1 horror. In a class full of light, who knew what devil would be roaming? Miss Blackfree was part devil on the inside but looked human on the outside. She's a maths teacher. Miss Blackfree picked me to do the question. It was 2 minus 1. I put the answer as 0. I know now it is 1. That fact haunts me to this day. Number 1 is the worst.

Declan Nixon (11)
Unity College, Towneley Holmes

Unlucky Number 7

I was number 7. Everyone says that the number 7 is a lucky number, however, I disagree. You see it was a lovely day and I had a swimming race and I was number 7 in the 7th row and the 7th round of swimmers. I heard my coach saying, "1... 2... 3... go!" I dived into the cold pool and swam as fast as I could but everything went black.
I woke up in the hospital with the doctors examining me. They didn't explain anything, they just sent me home with a 77 pound bill.

Rylee Walker (11)
Unity College, Towneley Holmes

6... 6... 6...

That's how long it is till 'it'. But what? you may ask. Months, years, I can't tell... You've heard the 666 thing? It might be cursed or fake? Well it is real. So real it can drag me to my death. With this mission I have to step inside. After 666 seconds, I whisper to myself, "1 more step..." over and over again.
I slip. I'm getting dragged... Help! That idiot is trying to get rid of me. That idiot Karl.
I'm dying...

Hasnain Shah (12)
Unity College, Towneley Holmes

The Mysterious Door!

It was 2099 when me and my friend Bisma found a spectacular rug in my garage. Intrigued, we took a closer look. It was like we got hypnotised from the pattern. Suddenly a gust of wind pushed the rug to the side. I noticed there was a huge hole in the cracked white tiles. Cautiously, I dangled my foot over the edge of the hole, I saw a rusty-looking door. The door creaked open. Someone inside bellowed, "2099, 2099, 2099!"

Mya Simpson (11)
Unity College, Towneley Holmes

YOUNG WRITERS INFORMATION

We hope you have enjoyed reading this book – and that you will continue to in the coming years.

If you're the parent or family member of an enthusiastic poet or story writer, do visit our website **www.youngwriters.co.uk/subscribe** and sign up to receive news, competitions, writing challenges and tips, activities and much, much more! There's lots to keep budding writers motivated!

If you would like to order further copies of this book, or any of our other titles, then please give us a call or order via your online account.

Young Writers
Remus House
Coltsfoot Drive
Peterborough
PE2 9BF
(01733) 890066
info@youngwriters.co.uk

Join in the conversation!
Tips, news, giveaways and much more!

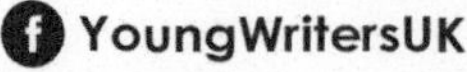

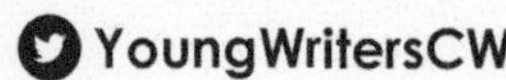

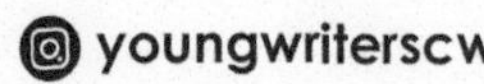

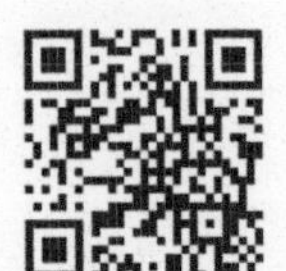

Scan me to watch the Integer video!